AF241818

A World We Never Knew

Faith

D. R. Long

drlongwrites.com

A World We Never Knew: Faith

For information, contact:

D. R. Long

drlongwrites.com | contact@drlongwrites.com

ISBN: 978-1-971469-06-5 (paperback)

ISBN: 978-1-971469-05-8 (ebook)

Cover design and editing by K. Jones and D. R. Long

Other Books by D. R. Long

Slimbies: Girl

A World We Never Knew: Chance

The Monsters We Are

ASL is not just a language,

it's a community.

A Letter to the Reader:

I used to think the hardest part of writing was finding the words.

Now I know it's learning to live with what they leave behind.

I've been inside this world too long... Long enough to feel its cold under my own skin. Each story takes something with it. A little light, a little faith. I tell myself it's worth it, that someone has to keep the record straight. But some nights I can't tell if I'm documenting what happened, or inventing a way to make it hurt less.

Faith isn't a story about miracles. It's about moving forward, one small, stubborn step after another. She walks through a world that offers her nothing and still keeps walking. I think that's what faith really is: not belief, but refusal. The quiet insistence that there's still something worth reaching for, even when you can't see it anymore.

When I started writing these, I thought each one would bring me closer to understanding why the world disappeared. Instead, it just feels farther away. Every page opens a door I didn't mean to build. Every ending sounds more like an echo than an answer.

Still, I keep going. Maybe... that's my kind of faith.

— D. R.

Act 1

Every story about the Vanishing starts with silence...
Then a hum...
Then the world forgets what the noise is for.

Chapter 1

Faith was strong, stronger than most girls her age. Not strong in the physical sense. She stood barely a hair over five feet. She had thick wavy dark hair, bright green eyes, olive skin, and didn't look like she could fight her way out of a mild breeze.

The bell had rung ten minutes ago, but the air still shook with movement. Doors burst open, kids spilling onto the steps in waves. Laughing, shoving, hollering the way kids do when a year finally ends.

Faith leaned against the sunbaked brick and felt them more than she saw them. Every heel-strike, every shriek, every slammed locker trembled through the wall into her shoulder blades. The building vibrated like a heartbeat.

She checked her phone. No message. There never was. Rita was always late.

Faith scrolled through old texts while the crowd thinned. Her father's messages scrolled past. Little check-ins, a picture of a hangar, a signed goodnight captured on video. Mixed between them were Rita's: sharp, abrupt, unfinished sentences that ended in dots or nothing at all.

She slid down the wall, jacket folded under her. The ground still shook from the running feet of kids escaping summer school letters and overdue grades. Someone's backpack hit the pavement with a thud she felt through her shoes.

She breathed the smell of asphalt, sunscreen, hot metal. A SEPTA bus rumbled past the corner, making the bricks vibrated faintly behind her.

She closed her eyes for a second, palms flat on the ground.

She didn't know it yet, but it was the last time she'd ever feel the school this alive.

Faith checked her phone again. 4:12 p.m.

She opened the video app and set her phone down on her backpack like a desk in front of her. The moment his face filled the screen, the world around her faded.

Geno smiled, the corners of his eyes creasing. His uniform collar sat open, hangar lights glinting off metal scaffolds behind him. A blur of movement crossed the far end of the frame. Other mechanics, a cart rolling by, but Faith barely noticed.

"Hey there, baby girl." His hands moved slow, deliberate, clear. Like he was still unsure himself.

Faith grinned and signed back fast, her fingers a little messy with excitement. "Hey, Dad. You working late again?"

He nodded, exaggerated for her. "Couple engines left to run. Then I'm done. You ready for tomorrow?"

"Always." She tucked a strand of hair behind her ear and leaned closer to the screen.

He told her about an engine that refused to start until he figured out a wiring short. She told him finals were finished. They traded small jokes, hands flying.

While they talked, the crowd around the school thinned to nothing. Faith didn't feel the rumble of footsteps anymore, didn't notice the bus pulling out at the corner. The air had gone still. All she saw was her father's hands, bright in the hangar light, shaping words only she could feel.

"Text me later, okay? Proud of you."

Faith turned toward the street as the horn blared again, long and sharp, lights flashing against the glass doors. She hadn't felt the first few blasts, she was too focused on her father's hands, but this one rattled the window beside her.

She looked up and saw the car idling crooked across two spaces. Rita's arm waved out the driver's window, bracelets jangling, mouth already moving a mile a minute. A few parents turned to stare. The teachers ignored it as if they were used to it.

Faith sighed, shoulders tightening. She lifted her phone, the video still open. "Hold on," she told her dad. She pointed the camera toward the street so he could see for himself. Geno's face softened. "She's early," he joked.

Faith smiled, small and tired. "No. She's mad. She's always mad."

Another blast of the horn. Rita's voice reached even through the closed glass, fragments of shape Faith knew by memory. Her mouth forming the words "lazy, waiting, can't you see me?"

Faith turned the phone back to her. "I have to go."

Geno nodded once, the smile fading but gentle. "Be good, okay? Tomorrow, nine o'clock. Same place."

"Promise."

"Love you, baby girl."

She signed it back quickly "Love you too" and pressed the screen dark.

The car horn went off again before her fingers left the glass.

Rita's voice hit like a punch before Faith even opened the door. Her mother's words always hit that way, blunt and physical.

"You'll get your time tomorrow! Hang up! And use your damn voice!"

Heads turned in the pickup line. Parents freezing mid-conversation, a teacher pretending to study her clipboard. The car idled half-crooked at the curb, window down, one arm waving wildly as Rita half-signed, half-shouted words that Faith already knew by shape.

Faith's throat tightened. The air felt thick, every breath catching in her chest. She clutched her phone like a lifeline.

"I'm sorry," she managed. The words came out thin, uneven.

Rita leaned closer across the seat, still shouting even though the glass was open. "What was that?"

Faith tried again, louder this time, the sound scraping from her throat. "I'm sorry." The words felt wrong in her mouth, thick and slurred, like her tongue was a stranger.

"You sound like you've got a damn foot in your mouth," Rita barked. "It's disgusting. How do you expect anyone to take you seriously talking like that?"

Faith's face burned. She climbed into the passenger seat, pulling the door shut before more of the world could look at her.

Rita was still going, her hands slicing through the air as she merged into traffic. "Every time you make me wait, every single time, it's always the same. I'm the one holding everything together while you sit around day-dreaming."

Faith stared down at her lap, phone clutched between her knees. The vibration of the road buzzed up through the seat, drowning out her mother's voice but never fully muting it.

Rita's words kept coming, spilling faster than the tires against the asphalt.

Rita slammed the car into gear, bracelets clattering against the wheel. "You think he's gonna care? You think that man gives a damn if you talk or not? He walked out when you were born,

Faith. Because of you. Because you came out broken and he couldn't handle it. And now I've got to waste my whole weekend driving you down there like some taxi service."

Rita kept going, words sharp as obsidian. "Court says he gets you one weekend a month. That's all he ever wanted. A little free time to play perfect daddy while I clean up what's left."

The light ahead turned green. Rita hit the gas hard, the car lurching forward. "You remember that when you see him. Remember who's really stuck with you."

Faith watched the city slide past the window, everything tilting and trembling with each turn.

The car whipped through traffic, Rita's voice filling the space between every stoplight. Bills, rent, gas, Geno. Everything came out in one long exhale that never seemed to end.

"I should've taken him for everything," she said, words sharp enough to slice the air. "All those years fixing planes, all that overtime and what's he even got to show for it? A base apartment and a kid he doesn't know what to do with."

Faith stared out the window, her reflection ghosted over the moving city. The afternoon light stretched long across the buildings, turning the glass gold. She didn't look at her mother, didn't sign, didn't move. She just watched the rhythm of the street pass by. She was trying to let the feeling of the car pull her away.

Engines shuddered through her seat. The window buzzed as she pressed her forehead against it. She felt the city more than she saw it, the pulse of it, the uneven hum under everything.

A green light blinked ahead. Rita cursed at someone that she cut off and hit the gas.

Faith pressed her head against the glass again, feeling the vibration of the tires over the uneven road. The gaps in traffic closed again, just as quickly as they'd opened.

Rita kept talking, but Faith didn't feel any of it anymore. She closed her eyes so she could ignore the motion.

The apartment felt smaller every time they walked in. Heat pressed in from the windows, thick enough to taste. Two cats prowled across the counter as Rita tossed her purse onto the table, the strap knocking an empty cup to the floor.

"Make dinner," she said, already kicking her shoes off. "I don't care what. I'm starving."

Faith set her backpack down quietly, signing, "I have homework."

Rita yanked a drawer open, silverware rattling. "You have chores."

Faith nodded once and crossed to the fridge. Inside, half a jar of sauce, two eggs, and a pack of noodles waited. She started boiling water. The burner's hum buzzed faintly through the counter under her palms.

Rita leaned against the wall, arms crossed, watching. "You know, he never had to do this kind of crap. Geno got everything easy. He never had to raise a broken kid by himself."

Faith stirred the noodles, letting the vibration of the spoon scrape through the pot. She didn't sign anything back.

When dinner hit the table, Rita took one bite and grimaced. "Too soft. You can't even cook pasta right?"

Faith signed, "Sorry."

Rita's eyes narrowed. "Use your words."

Faith swallowed, throat tight. "I'm sorry," she said, the sound catching on the first syllable.

Rita smirked, satisfied, and went back to her phone. The screen light flickered across her face, messages sent to someone labeled Geno (work). None of them showed replies.

They ate in silence, just the scrape of forks and the faint vibration of traffic through the floor. One of the cats jumped onto Faith's chair, brushed against her leg, and disappeared again.

When the dishes were done, Faith signed, "Goodnight," and slipped down the short hallway to her room. She could feel the vibrations of her mother's yelling through the walls still. Faith hoped she wouldn't come in to yell more tonight.

The air in her room felt heavier but quieter. She lay back on the narrow bed, phone glowing in her hand. Her father's last message sat at the top: Text me when you get home safe.

She typed, "Home. Love you," and hit send.

The screen dimmed, and the world shrank to the hum of pipes and the thump of a cat landing somewhere overhead. She closed her eyes thinking of her father's promise. "Tomorrow, 9 am."

It wasn't peace exactly. Just quiet.

And it was the last quiet night the world would ever have.

Chapter 2

Morning sun slid between the high-rises, flashing off the windshields ahead. The car's low rumble pressed through the floorboards. Faith kept her shoes off, toes curled against the vibration. It was one of the few sensations she trusted to stay the same.

Rita drove like she always did, one hand on the wheel, the other guarding a gas-station coffee. The Bluetooth light blinked uselessly beside her. She was talking again, half to herself, half to whoever might be listening.

"…traffic's worse every damn day… court should've never given him weekends… bills are late again…"

Faith caught the rhythm of her mother's jaw more than the words. The shapes moved fast, angry, almost familiar but not directed at her. She leaned her head against the window and let the glass buzz against her temple. The hum of the A/C pulsed through the dash, a soft breeze under her fingers.

Outside, the world drifted past in layers. Steel guardrails, green highway signs, a thousand cars inching toward somewhere. Heat shimmered above the asphalt like a living thing.

Her phone lit and buzzed on her lap.

Dad - Dover AFB: Leaving the hangar. See you soon, kiddo.

Faith smiled at her phone, but before the expression faded, Rita's eyes flicked to the rearview mirror, sharp as a blade. Faith didn't type back. She just locked the screen and turned it face-down on her thigh.

The traffic crawled. Lights flickered in rear view mirrors, silent flashes of color. Faith closed her eyes again, feeling each start and stop through the seatbelt's slow tightening across her chest.

Everything felt ordinary. Heavy, bright, predictable.

Ten minutes crawled by in fits and jerks. The highway should've been a parking lot, but the rhythm kept changing. Stop, surge, sudden gaps like someone had lifted pieces off the board.

Faith blinked, watching the line of cars ahead stretch and thin in perfect intervals. Too even. Too clean.

Rita's hand drummed on the wheel. "Finally," she muttered, "people moving like they've got somewhere to be for once."

Faith pressed her palm to the window. The vibration under her hand stuttered, the constant bass of engines ahead dropping out for a beat, then returning weaker, emptier.

Another few seconds and the pattern broke again. Her stomach fluttered with each pause, like missing steps on a staircase.

She signed, "Cars… gone."

Rita waved her off without looking. "They're just idiots slamming brakes."

But Faith kept watching. A white sedan in the middle lane flickered once, like a heat mirage swallowing it whole. A pickup behind it swerved, clipped another fender. Metal twisted and shrieked in the lane beside her, but she only felt the scream of metal through her seat.

The dashboard clock changed.

8:03 A.M.

Faith's fingers tightened on the seat belt.

A motorcycle buzzed up the shoulder, whipping past mirrors. For a moment its engine vibrated strong against the car frame, the pulse steady under Faith's feet. Then it stopped.

No crash, no slide, nothing in the mirror but a strip of empty asphalt.

Rita cursed at the drivers around them, gesturing at the wreckage up ahead. "Nobody knows how to fuckin' drive anymore?!"

Faith didn't answer. She could feel the absence. The world still running, but parts of it missing beats, like a song skipping on repeat.

The morning glare sharpened, white and metallic. For a heartbeat it looked like sunlight catching on chrome, then the world ahead bloomed into fire.

A tanker near the bend went up. The explosion didn't roar so much as hit. The pressure slammed through the windshield, a solid thing that punched Faith's chest and rattled her teeth. She gasped, clutching the seatbelt.

Heat flashed across the hood. Rita screamed something Faith couldn't read, the car jerking hard as she stomped the brake.

Faith's palms pressed to the dash. The vibration changed. It wasn't the steady hum of engines in tandem... It was chaos. Some frequencies vanished, others spiked. The road itself seemed to shake.

Half the cars ahead vanished. One blink, then emptiness where metal should've been. Others swerved in panic, drivers yanking wheels into barriers or each other. Faith watched one woman in the passenger seat of a passing car mouth a scream as she realized nobody was driving her vehicle.

The air felt wrong, vacant, hollow. Faith could feel the suction of it, pressure bending through the frame as if space had hiccupped.

Rita's coffee shot across the dash and burst against the vent. She shrieked, twisting the wheel, trying to steer through the smoke and debris.

Faith stared past her mother's shoulder. The tanker's remains burned a hundred yards ahead, flames bending in a wind that didn't touch anything else. Cars disappeared mid-spin, others stopped dead, doors hanging open.

A sedan ahead flipped onto its roof, sliding toward them. Rita swerved, the tires skidding over shattered glass. The car jolted sideways, and Faith's world went weightless for half a second.

The heat faded as quickly as it came, leaving only light and dust.

Rita's knuckles were white on the steering wheel, eyes wide and unblinking.

"What the hell just happened?" she mouthed, but Faith didn't answer.

The hum had died.

Everything was still.

They sat motionless in the middle lane, steam curling from the hood.

Faith's pulse pounded against the seat belt, every beat echoing through the metal frame.

Rita's hands shook on the wheel. "Okay," she whispered, more to herself than anyone. "Okay, we're fine. We're fine."

A horn wailed somewhere around them. Faith felt it through her feet before she saw it.

The tanker came sideways down the grade, trailer skidding broadside across three lanes. Its tires screamed, leaving black ribbons on the asphalt. Through the windshield Faith saw the driver's face, mouth open in a silent yell.

Rita froze.

Faith didn't. She screamed, folding into herself, arms over her head, knees pulled tight against her chest. The vibration built to a roar she could feel in her bones.

Closer...

CLOSER...

And then nothing.

No impact. No shudder. Just stillness.

Faith's breath hitched. She lifted her head slowly.

The road was empty.

Only the tire marks remained, fresh and smoking, curling gray against the pavement where the truck had been.

Rita stared at them, eyes wide, lips trembling. "What the fuck is going on?"

She slammed her palm against the wheel and stomped the gas. The tires caught, the car jerking forward.

For a moment the world felt hollow, drained of every hum Faith had ever known. Then, behind them, came the dull vibration of other engines colliding. Small, scattered crashes, chaos rebuilding itself.

Faith gripped the door handle as they sped through the wreckage, steam and dust rising around them like ghosts.

Rita took the first exit she saw, tires bumping over the curb. The ramp curved down into the city, smoke hanging low between the buildings.

They crept forward through wreckage. Cars burned at odd angles, doors hanging open, others just… empty. Storefront glass glittered across the sidewalks. Somewhere distant, an alarm blinked but made no sound Faith could feel.

Rita's knuckles were bone white on the wheel. She whispered under her breath, half-prayers, half-curses, every word shaking.

Faith kept her eyes outside. A bus leaned against a light pole, windows blown out, seats still full of bags and jackets. A man stood in the street waving for help, and then he wasn't. No flash, no smoke. Just gone. No clothes, no screams, no man.

She pressed her palm to the window. The glass vibrated faintly with the car's idle. Across the intersection, a mother and her son clung to each other. The boy reached for her hand and reached through air as she vanished from his grip.

Rita flinched at something ahead, jerking the wheel around a stalled truck. "We'll go home," she said, her voice rising like she was talking herself up. "It'll be fine there. Home's fine."

Faith tried to sign, but Rita was locked on the road. She swallowed and let the words choke in her throat. "Mom, I'm scared."

She saw Rita mouth the words "me too, Faith," followed by the shape of several swear words.

They passed an overpass where a car had torn through the guardrail and hung nose-down, wheels still spinning in the void below. Steam rose from the gaps in the pavement like the city itself was exhaling.

Faith's fingers trembled as she unlocked her phone. The screen lit bright against the gray light.

No Service.

She tried again. Nothing.

The hum of the world was quieter now. Thinner, off-beat, like something missing from a song she'd always known.

Faith set the phone in her lap and watched the dying city slide by, feeling the vibration fade until there was almost nothing left.

Chapter 3

Smoke hung low over the streets, thick enough to tint the morning gold. Rita drove with both hands locked on the wheel, her eyes darting between every shadow. They wound through intersections where the lights still worked, changing color for no one. A SEPTA bus blocked one lane, doors yawning open, empty seats still holding purses and jackets. The engine ticked faintly beneath the hood, a mechanical heartbeat that hadn't learned the world was gone.

Faith kept her palm against the window. The city vibrated wrong, too slow, uneven. What little traffic remained crawled in stutters: a car rolling driverless until it hit a pole, a bike laid across a crosswalk. She felt each motion as a dull tremor through the glass, like the city's rhythm was breaking apart one beat at a time.

"Where is everyone?" Faith signed. She looked inside vehicles and buildings, expecting to see mouths screaming, bodies broken and dead in the streets. But there was nothing.

No people.

No bodies.

No screaming.

It was all just... gone.

A billboard ahead flashed ads for concerts that would never happen. Rita muttered at it under her breath, words Faith couldn't catch, maybe prayers, maybe curses.

They passed Market Street. A child's stroller sat in the center lane, wheels still spinning in the hot wind. Faith's chest tightened; she looked away before it stopped. "Mom, I'm scared," she signed.

"Me too," Rita finally exhaled. "Almost there," she said, voice small and hoarse. "Just… almost there."

Faith nodded, then refocused her eyes on the buildings sliding by. Windows blackened, doors hanging open, curtains fluttering in rooms with no one left to pull them closed.

At the corner, the car slowed. Their block waited ahead, half-hidden in dust and heat shimmer.

Rita pressed the gas again. The tires crunched over broken glass. The closer they got, the less the world seemed to move.

Rita pulled the car to the curb and killed the engine. Faith unbuckled and stepped out. The heat hit immediately, thick with the stench of smoke and gasoline.

The street looked half erased. Cars tilted against hydrants, glass scattered like ice. A city bus had driven straight into the corner of their building, its front end buried in brick. Flames licked through the shattered windows, coughing black smoke into the sky.

For a second, Faith just stared. The whole block leaned wrong, like gravity had shifted. Their apartment still stood, the top half warped but holding, curtains flapping through broken windows.

Rita slammed the car door and stood beside her, one hand shading her eyes. "It's fine," she said quickly, too quickly. "Our side's fine. We'll grab what we need and go."

Faith's hands moved before she thought. "It's not safe."

Rita didn't even look at her. "It's fine," she repeated, already moving toward the steps.

Faith hesitated. The fire popped somewhere above them, glass cracking in the heat. She could feel it in the air, the soft vibration of her whole world falling apart.

Rita was halfway up the stairs when she turned back. "Faith, come on."

Faith followed, slow, eyes darting to the smoldering bus below. The metal ticked as it cooled, tiny vibrations running through the concrete under her feet.

By the time she reached the landing, Rita was already at their door, keys in hand, jamming the lock that no longer mattered.

"See?" Rita said. "Still standing."

Faith didn't answer. The building creaked overhead, dust falling like ash. She signed again, smaller this time. "Not for long."

Rita pushed the door open. "Then hurry."

The door pushed open against swollen wood, catching halfway before giving way. For a moment, the place almost looked normal.

Clothes scattered across the couch. A lamp on its side. Plates still on the table where they'd eaten last night. Cats slipped between shadows, tails puffed, eyes wide and glassy.

Rita moved fast, drawers flying open, closet door slamming back against the wall. Each impact sent a dull vibration through the floor. She pointed toward Faith's room, mouthing words Faith didn't need to read to understand. "Clothes. Chargers. Anything worth something."

Faith crossed to her room, breath shallow. The floor trembled faintly under her steps, not enough to shake balance, but enough to send chills down her arms. She grabbed her backpack, stuffed a few shirts inside, then picked up the photo of her father from the dresser. The glass was cracked, but his smile still held.

Something shifted nearby, a faint tremor through the wall, rhythmic, alive.

Faith turned toward it, her hand tracing the vibration into the next bedroom. The door hung half off its hinges. She pushed it open, and dust rolled out in a warm wave that burned her throat.

The wall had started to cave in from the neighboring apartment. One of their cats lay pinned beneath a fallen shelf, hind legs twitching weakly. Its mouth opened again and again, silent cries forming shapes she could almost feel in her chest.

Faith dropped to her knees, stretching against the door and wall, trying to lift the edge of the shelf. It shifted slightly but held fast. The wood quivered under her grip.

Rita appeared in the doorway, face flushed from heat and effort. Her hand sliced the air in an impatient gesture, "Leave it."

Faith shook her head, signed quickly, "It's ours."

Rita stepped forward, grip iron-tight on her arm. Her lips moved sharply, anger in every line of her face. Faith didn't need to read the words.

She tried one last time, muscles trembling, dust stinging her eyes. The shelf shuddered. Cracks spider webbed across the wall. Plaster dust drifted down in a slow gray curtain.

Rita yanked her back just as part of the wall gave way. The shelf collapsed with a heavy thud that she felt through the soles of her shoes.

They stumbled into the hallway. Faith blinked through the haze and signed small, "I'm sorry."

Rita was already scooping things into a bag, jaw set hard. She pointed toward the door, her lips mouthing, "Move."

Faith followed, each step shaking with the vibrations of the dying building.

Rita wiped sweat from her forehead and looked down the hall. The wallpaper curled from the heat, flakes of paint drifting like ash. "They always had money," her mouth shaped, eyes bright with something that wasn't fear.

Faith signed fast. "We should go."

Rita shook her head, already pressing her shoulder against the next door. The swollen frame gave way with a jolt that Faith felt through the floorboards.

Inside, the air was thicker, dust hanging in sunlight like smoke under water.

Rita pointed toward a narrow space where two beams had fallen together, blocking most of the doorway. Her hands moved sharply, "In there. Grab what you can."

Faith hesitated. The air trembled with each breath of the building. She signed again, slower this time. "It's falling."

Rita gestured harder, "Hurry up! I won't fit!"

Faith dropped to her knees and crawled through. The gap scraped her shoulders; splinters caught in her hair. Just enough light to slice through floating dust. Every movement made the ceiling above her shiver.

She lost sight of Rita in the dust and mess behind, crawling until she found the master bedroom in the back corner of the apartment. Broken picture frames leaned against the wall, glass glittering. A small plastic truck lay half buried in debris. And across the room, a dresser.

She reached the dresser, heart hammering. The floor vibrated in uneven pulses, something heavy shifting in the walls. A jewelry box sat open on the dresser, necklaces spilled across it. She stuffed the jewelry into her jacket pocket, gold and costume pieces clinking together.

Behind her, she felt the faint tremor of Rita pounding the wall. When she reappeared, her mother's mouth moved like it was shouting, but Faith couldn't hear a thing.

The vibrations deepened. Plaster drifted down in a soft rain. The flashlight flickered once.

Faith hurried, crawling fast now, the dust choking her throat. A deep shudder rippled through the floor; long, low, and wrong. The ceiling cracked open, dropping pieces the size of her head.

She dove through the narrow gap just as the doorway sagged inward. A beam crashed where she'd been seconds earlier, thudding hard enough that the impact jumped through her palms.

Rita caught her by the wrist and yanked her upright, coughing, eyes wide but dry. Her lips formed the words "See? Fine. You're fine."

Faith didn't answer, just sobbed. The whole hallway was tilting slightly now, dust curling in the sunlight.

Rita adjusted her grip, pulled her toward the stairs. "Come on. Let's get out of here."

Faith glanced back once, the apartment billowing dust, the flicker of flames and shadows dancing on the walls.

They carried what they could. Rita's arms were loaded with trash bags that dragged and tore against the steps, metal zippers and picture frames clattering inside. Faith had only her backpack, straps heavy on her shoulders.

Outside, the heat was worse. The flames from the building had grown. The bus that had struck the corner still hissed, its tires slowly melting into the asphalt. The air shimmered, thick with the smell of plastic and gas.

Rita dropped the bags beside the car, breathing hard. "Go on, get in," her mouth shaped, impatience in the sharp snap of her wrist.

Faith climbed into the passenger seat, buckled the belt automatically. Rita slid in after her, ripped one of the bags open, and sifted through the mix of clothes and trinkets.

She stuck her hand out, demanding the jewelry Faith had found. She snatched it, chains tangled together, metal flashing dull in the light.

"This all?" Rita's lips curved, half-snarl, half-smile. "Whatever. We'll find more."

Faith turned toward the building. Their windows were gone now, flames breathing through the holes like lungs. Curtains flared and vanished.

She signed small against her lap. "Where will we go?"

Rita's eyes moved to the road ahead. "Don't worry," she said. "We'll find someplace better. Who's going to stop us?"

Faith looked back through the rear window as they pulled away. The apartment sagged inward, swallowed by its own smoke. Somewhere beyond the burning skyline, she imagined her father still out there, waiting to come and rescue her.

The hum beneath the tires followed them out of the city, uneven but steady, the last heartbeat of home fading behind them.

Chapter 4

The sun settled behind the haze of smoke, smearing the Philadelphia skyline in rust and ash. A motel crouched off the highway, THE MAPLE INN. Half its letters had burned out, the remaining ones blinked red and sputtered, VACANCY sign flashing.

Rita slowed the car and pulled into the cracked lot. A dozen cars sat scattered across it, some with doors hanging open, others still idling faintly though no one was behind the wheel. Another had found itself in the window of room 113, next to it a suitcase had burst, clothes covered with dust.

Faith pressed her hand to the window as they rolled past. The air trembled with the low pulse of electricity. The steady rhythm thumped up through her shoes when the car stopped, like a heartbeat buried underground. It was the first thing she'd felt that wasn't chaos.

Rita exhaled hard, killing the engine. "See?" she said, lips curling into something that almost looked like satisfaction.

"People left everything behind. We can take what we need." Faith watched her lips and nodded.

Faith looked around the lot again. The stillness pressed in, heavy and airless. No footsteps. No tremor of movement. Nothing alive. She stared at the cars, the open doors, the still blinking motel sign. The world had cracked in half this morning, but the ground here was clean.

She turned toward Rita, signing, "Where is everyo-"

Rita didn't answer. She was already out of the car, heels crunching over gravel as she moved toward the office.

Faith's hand hovered mid-sign, unfinished. She thought again of the people on the highway. How they hadn't died, they didn't scream, how they'd simply vanished, leaving nothing but motion and fire behind.

Rita banged on the motel office door. "Hello? Anybody home?"

No one answered. She glanced back, then waved Faith forward, already twisting the knob. The lock clicked open without a fight. "See?" Rita mouthed, stepping inside. "Told you. Luck's finally turning."

Faith hesitated beside the car, one last glance sweeping the empty road. The air smelled faintly of melted plastic and impending rain. Then she followed her mother toward the humming light.

Rita pushed through the office door like she owned it. The little bell above it shook once and hung crooked. Papers littered the counter, a phone blinking red with missed messages. A family's worth of luggage sat by a bench off to one side.

She moved behind the desk, sliding open drawers, scooping bills from the register into her pocket. "Shame to let all this go to waste," her mouth shaped, more to herself than to Faith.

A pegboard hung on the wall, dozens of keys still dangling. Rita ran her hand across them, the plastic tags clicking together. "One-oh-four," she decided, plucking it loose.

Beside the counter, a vending machine hummed quietly, lights steady behind the glass. Rita found the maintenance key in a drawer and twisted it open. Bags of chips and candy spilled into her tote, a can of soda clattering to the tile.

She looked at Faith, half-smiling, half-snapping. "See? People just walked out. Their loss."

Faith signed, small. "Why?"

Rita didn't look up. "Because they're stupid," she said aloud, scooping another handful of snacks. "Or scared. Or both."

Outside, the sky had turned a deeper red. Faith trailed her mother across the lot again, the rhythm of her heels tapping through the pavement. She followed to the room, the door creaking open on stiff hinges.

The air inside was stale and dry, heavy with the smell of dust and old carpet cleaner. Everything looked untouched. Bedspread flat, TV remote still in its plastic sheath, even a little mint on the pillows.

Rita dropped her bag on the bed and flipped the switch beside it. The lamp blinked on. The TV followed, soundless reruns flickering across the screen, people laughing with nobody there.

Faith sat on the edge of the other bed, eyes tracing the window. Outside, the parked cars still waited like loyal pets. Exhaust fumes making little heat shimmers behind the ones still running.

Rita scrolled through the channels until she found a pay-per-view menu. "Huh," she said, half-laughing. "Still works. Guess the world's not over after all." She clicked a title, a bright-colored comedy with canned laughter, and threw herself onto the bed with a bag of chips.

"See?" she said, crunching loud, crumbs catching at the corner of her mouth. "People'll be back. You'll see. Things go to hell, then they fix themselves. They always do."

Faith didn't answer, barely noticed the vibrations coming from her mother. She kept her eyes on the glass, her reflection caught between the window's glare and the dim blue glow of the TV.

Behind her, Rita kept talking through mouthfuls of food. "Your dad's probably hiding under a plane somewhere. Figures he'd disappear when people that need him actually need him."

The line hung in the room. Faith kept her eyes on the world outside.

Outside, the sign across the lot blinked VACANCY steadily.

The movie had long since ended, leaving the TV to loop its menu screen in pale blue light. Rita lay sprawled across one of the beds, chip bag spilled across her shirt, soft snores breaking the still rhythm of the room.

Faith sat by the window, chin on her knees, watching the empty parking lot below. The night air buzzed through the air conditioner, its constant tremor running up her legs through the metal chair. It was steady. Predictable.

She liked that. Even if it was chilly.

The lot hadn't changed since they arrived. Cars sat where people had left them, one with its engine still humming faintly. Nothing moved. Not even the curtains in the other rooms.

She pressed her palm to the glass, feeling the machine hum behind the wall, when a sudden vibration broke the pattern. Sharper, louder. The lamp rattled once on the nightstand and the light flickered.

Faith turned. The radio on the dresser had flicked to life.

It was one of those old brown models, fake wood siding, red numbers glowing dull. Static rolled through it, the kind she could feel more than hear. It shivered the air in uneven bursts, a pulse that didn't belong. The numbers rolled like it was possessed.

She crossed the room, barefoot on the rough carpet, and set her hand on the top of the radio. The casing buzzed beneath her fingertips. Erratic, uneven, but somehow alive.

The static changed. Slow, rhythmic. Not random.

Her fingers traced the beat like reading Braille.

Then, between each pulse, something formed...

Vowels...

Breath...

Sound.

"Faith…"

Her eyes went wide. She felt the word inside her chest, not against her skin. The world around her went weightless.

"Faith… stay calm…"

Tears welled instantly. Her throat clenched; she pressed both hands flat on the radio now, desperate to keep the connection.

"Stay inside."

It was a man's voice. Warm, sure, gentle in the way people rarely were with her. She didn't recognize it by sound, but something in her knew.

It was her father.

The air conditioner cut out. The whole room held its breath.

Faith did too.

A sob broke from her throat, quiet, startled. She clapped her hand over her mouth, not wanting to lose the moment.

"Stay strong, Faith."

The voice stuttered once, fading into a long hiss. Static climbed higher, vibrating through the floorboards. The lamp rattled again, harder.

Rita stirred in the other bed.

Faith kept her hands pressed to the radio, her voice scratching against her throat as she pleaded to no one, "Please, come back!"

The static surged like a wave, bright and physical, almost too loud to feel.

Rita jerked awake, sitting upright before she knew why. The room glowed blue from the TV. Faith stood in front of the dresser, hands shaking, tears streaking her face. Static roared from the radio, far louder than the tiny speaker should be.

"It's Dad!" she said, voice raw and uneven, the words dragging out of her throat like they'd never been used. "It's Dad! On the radio!"

Rita blinked at the sound, at her daughter's voice, and then toward the radio where only static rolled in soft waves. She squinted, rubbed her eyes. "What are you talking about?"

Faith turned, signing and speaking both now, frantic. "It's him! He's talking! I heard him!"

"Why is this even on? Turn this off!" Rita's face twisted. She reached across the bed, yanked the cord from the wall. The static didn't stop. It just deepened, a low, endless hiss that made the lamp tremble.

Rita shook the radio hard, shouting over the hissing radio, "There's nothing there! It's just static!"

Faith stumbled forward, still crying, still signing. "It's Dad! It's Dad!"

The slap cracked through the room.

For a second neither of them moved.

Faith's cheek burned; her hands hung halfway to her chest, trembling.

Rita's breath steadied. Her voice came out cold. "It's not your fucking father. You can't even hear, how would you know what he sounds like? He abandoned us, dummy. He's gone like the rest of them."

She threw the radio across the room. It hit the wall, fell hard, cords tangled.

The static kept going.

"Stupid fucking radio batteries..." Rita froze for half a heartbeat, then turned away, smoothing the chips from the blanket like nothing had happened.

Faith stood there a moment longer, fingers pressed against her cheek.

The radio popped once, a sharp pulse that shook the air, and then went silent.

"There, see, it's stopped," Rita said as she laid down, turning her back to Faith. "Now shut up and go to sleep."

She moved slowly, crawling carefully into her bed quietly trying not to make the bedsprings squeak. Her cheek still burned where the slap had landed. She touched it once, then pulled her hand away like it stung all over again.

Faith sat perfectly still until Rita's breathing evened out again. She watched the soft rise and fall of her chest under the blue light of the TV that seemed to wash everything flat and colorless.

The radio lay on its side against the wall, a hairline crack splitting the fake wood. Its red numbers still glowed faintly.

She pulled the blanket over her head and bit the edge of it to stop her whimpers from escaping, shoulders shaking.

The hum from the air conditioner filled the space around her. She focused on that, the steady vibration against the blanket, the only thing that didn't hurt.

Her tears slid down onto the pillow, hot, then cold. She stayed as still as she could, each breath measured, quiet, until her body gave out.

By the time sleep took her, the room had gone still again, as if nothing had ever happened at all.

Chapter 5

Faith woke to thin yellow light pressing through the curtains that felt too warm for morning. Her cheek throbbed when she rolled onto it, a dull bruise blooming under the surface. It was still warm when she touched it.

She sat up slowly. Rita was already dressed, hair pulled back tight, pillowcase stretched wide in her hands as she dumped half a drawer's worth of snacks inside. The chip bag from last night crackled beneath her knee.

"Good," Rita's mouth shaped when she spotted Faith sitting up. "You're finally awake."

She tossed an empty pillowcase onto Faith's bed. "Get dressed and start going room to room. Anything valuable. Jewelry, money, food."

Her tone was brisk, practiced, like she'd given these same instructions for years. She didn't wait for Faith to get up, already walking the bag of snacks out the door. "Let's get moving! Riches won't find themselves!" Her words echoed off the walls unheard, her mouth kept moving, filling the room with words Faith would never hear.

Faith blinked sleep from her eyes, heart heavy. The air still smelled faintly of burnt plastic from outside, mixed with the stale scent of old carpet and yesterday's fear.

She pulled on her shoes and reached for her backpack immediately, the one thing she wouldn't leave in the room. She slipped the straps onto her shoulders, hugging them there for a moment like a shield. She knew Rita wouldn't think twice about leaving her bag behind.

Through the window, half the motel doors hung open. Rita had been up for a while, Faith could see her footsteps in the dust moving door to door, sweeping each room like a scavenger at a yard sale.

Faith stood, feeling the ache from the night settle deep in her chest. She opened the door. The morning hit her warm and humid, carrying no breeze, no movement at all. Just emptiness.

She paused on the threshold, backpack straps clutched in both fists.

Everyone she had ever loved was gone.

And she was still here.

With her.

Her cheek ached again as she clenched her jaw. She didn't touch it. She took a deep breath, dropped her eyes to the cracked pavement, and walked towards the nearest closed door.

Faith tried the first door on the motel row.

Locked.

She jiggled the handle once, twice, feeling the stubborn thud of it through her palm. She turned to scan the parking lot to see what Rita was doing.

Behind her, Rita stood in the lot with a hand on her hip, mouth curling into a smirk.

"They're locked, dummy," she mouthed, tapping her temple like Faith had forgotten something obvious. She pointed toward the office, laughing silently at her.

Faith's stomach tightened. She adjusted her backpack strap and walked back across the lot.

Inside the office, the pegboard still hung with rows of metal keys. She took the heaviest ring, a cluster of twenty, jingling softly against her palm.

Most of the rooms were empty. Beds unrumpled, curtains still drawn, a stillness clinging to them that felt wrong. Faith moved through them one by one, pillowcase at her hip, picking up whatever looked useful:

a half-filled bottle of water, a pack of gum, a couple loose dollar bills, a cracked travel brush, a pair of sunglasses.

Just enough to show Rita she'd done what she was told.

In the fourth room, a chair was tipped over and a suitcase lay half-open on the bed, clothes hanging out like someone had been packing when the world went silent. A child's shoe sat beside it. Tiny, pink, unworn.

Faith swallowed and kept moving.

The eighth room felt different the moment she stepped inside. Dust floated in the thin morning light, and the air smelled faintly of old perfume. On the nightstand sat a pocket watch.

Silver. Heavy.

Its hinge was cracked, but the engraving curled beautifully along the edges. Vines, initials faded with age. She picked it up and opened it carefully.

One side: empty, ready for a picture.

The other: a frozen second hand, stopped mid-tick.

She ran her thumb over the empty frame, the groove cool under her skin.

In the last room she checked, she closed the door gently behind her, set her pillowcase down, and unzipped her backpack.

Her father's picture lay inside, still in it's cracked frame. She held it a moment, thumb brushing the familiar smile. Tears stung the corners of her eyes, slow and hot.

She flipped it over, and pulled the picture out. "I'm sorry, Daddy," she mouthed silently. She ripped the picture carefully, tearing around the edges until it was small enough to fit the watch.

When she pressed the photo into the frame, it slid in perfectly, like it had been waiting for it.

She snapped the watch shut. The soft click felt final.

Faith tucked it deep into her jacket pocket, hiding it from sight. Deep in her pocket, there was a small rip where the watch would just slip through, knowing Rita would take it if she saw even a glint of silver. A tiny sob shook her shoulders, but she swallowed it back before it grew.

"Maybe he's still out there..." she thought to herself. But the voice from the radio echoed through her memory, warped and distant, and she wasn't sure if she believed it.

She wiped her face with the back of her sleeve, picked up the pillowcase, and stepped back out the door.

For the first time since the world ended, something inside her felt still.

Rita hauled the last overstuffed pillowcase to the trunk, humming a tuneless little rhythm under her breath. Not happy, just energized. Busy. Preoccupied with her own momentum.

"People just left everything behind," her mouth formed as she slammed the trunk. "Their loss. Our gain."

Faith didn't respond. She tightened her backpack straps and climbed into the passenger seat.

The lot around them sat baking under the early sun. Cars still dotted the spaces, some with doors yawning open, others frozen exactly where people had stepped away from them. A few engines still ran in low idle, their vibrations trembling faintly through the asphalt.

One sat close to the motel entrance, headlights dim, grille cracked. As Rita turned the key, Faith felt the tremor beside her flicker… then die. The engine sputtered, coughed once, and went silent. The heat shimmer behind it disappeared like breath wiped from glass.

Rita didn't notice. She was already checking mirrors, deciding on direction.

"North looks blocked," she muttered. "West will have nicer houses. Might as well live somewhere decent if the world is over."

Faith rested her palm against the door, feeling the steady rumble of their own car beneath her. The tires crunched over gravel as they rolled forward. In the rearview mirror, every open motel door hung crooked, curtains fluttering like someone had just stepped out and vanished mid-motion.

Faith watched them shrink behind her, the empty spaces where people had been. Where they should still be. Her fingers tightened around the strap of her backpack, the weight of the pocket watch pressing against her side.

They turned onto the road heading west. Lines of power poles swept past, humming their constant, steady rhythm overhead. Rita kept the car radio off, her hand resting protectively near the dial.

Faith didn't try to turn it on.

She didn't need to.

The memory of her father's voice still echoed inside her chest, the one place Rita couldn't reach.

The road curved toward the river, the sky behind them bruised with black smoke. Rita tightened her grip on the wheel as the bridge rose ahead, the long arch of it empty, stretching out like a dare.

Faith looked out the window, the city burned behind them in slow motion. Orange flickers licking through high windows, plumes of smoke curling upward like tired ghosts.

They rolled onto the bridge. The tires hummed, steady and even. Below, the water was murky with ash, thick as soup, the surface barely moving. Besides their car, the bridge was empty.

Rita scanned the far bank, where houses climbed the hills; wide porches, trimmed hedges, old stone faces. "See those?" she said, her lips pulling into a hungry smile. "Rich people homes. We can pick one. We can pick them all! Since the world's ended, we can live wherever we want. Let's try one of those."

Faith didn't answer. She turned back to the window and watched the line where the river met the burned skyline, her hand still flat on the glass.

A burst of static snapped through the speakers, sharp and violent, slamming through the seat into Faith's spine. Rita shrieked, jerking the wheel. The car skidded, tires screaming against concrete before she stomped the brakes.

Faith lurched forward, grabbing the dashboard. The static climbed, pulsing.

And then...

"Faith."

Her name. Clear. Warm. Impossible. She heard again, she heard him again.

Faith froze, breath locking in her throat. Her father's voice wrapped through her chest like a hand.

Rita's palm slapped the dial hard. The radio cut, the voice vanishing mid-syllable. Rita panted, other hand white on the wheel. "Fucking junk," she snapped. "Scared the hell out of me."

She glanced at Faith.

Faith had shrunk into herself, shoulders raised, eyes wide, bracing like a slap was coming.

Rita scoffed. "What? You think I'm gonna hit you again?" She shook her head, annoyed. "You didn't do this. Stupid old car." She brushed her hair back, already shifting her mood. "They're bound to have something better over there," she said, nodding toward the houses ahead.

She put the car back in gear, muttering under her breath as they rolled forward.

Faith stayed silent, one hand curled tight around the pocket watch hidden in her jacket. She turned her face toward the window, letting the cold glass steady her.

The bridge behind them looked empty, the city exhaled smoke across the river in silence. Ahead, the road stretched clean, like an unseen servant had swept the world just for them.

Act 2

Most survivors will tell you the world didn't stay gone...
That it just came back wrong.
If they only knew...

Chapter 6

The cold hit first.

Faith woke to it pressing against her cheeks, seeping through the blankets like the mansion itself was breathing frost. She curled closer to the warmth trapped under the covers, but the air still nipped at her nose and fingertips. When she finally forced herself to sit, a thin cloud of breath fogged in front of her mouth.

October.

She hated how loud the cold could feel.

The room around her was still dim. Pale morning light leaked through tall windows lined with dust, pooling across a floor that always seemed colder than the rest of the house. The mansion held cold the same way it held silence, deeply in its bones.

Faith swung her legs over the edge of the bed, rubbing warmth back into her arms. Her reflection in the tall mirror waited across the room, half-swallowed by shadow. She pushed herself to stand, padding across the frigid floorboards until her ghostly outline sharpened in the glass.

She didn't look older.

But she did look thinner.

Her collarbones showed more sharply, her cheeks a little hollow from four months of rationing. She wasn't starving, no… But Rita ate well enough for two. Faith had learned to take small portions, always leaving the bigger share behind. Her hair hung limper than it used to. Her eyes looked… quiet. Too quiet for fourteen.

She blinked at herself, then turned away and dug through the pile of clothes Rita had scavenged from upstairs closets. Mismatched sweaters. A man's button-down shirt two sizes too big. A pair of leggings with a hole at the knee. Nothing warm enough on its own. She pulled on layers until she looked like she'd been stuffed inside a thrift store donation box.

The hallway outside her room felt even colder. The stone under her socks drank her heat immediately. She moved down the long corridor, passing portraits whose faces had faded with dust and time. The mansion was always like this in the morning, a hollow shell pretending to be a home.

Downstairs, faint light warmed the wide foyer, golden and soft. The smell of stale coffee drifted through the air.

Rita sat in a velvet chair she'd dragged near the window, wrapped in one of the mansion's fur-lined robes. Her hair was brushed smooth for once. A half-empty mug rested on her knee, steam curling from it. She'd put on a little weight these past months. Not enough to be obvious, just a slight fullness in her face, her shoulders, her stomach. Comfort from stolen snacks and late-night wine bottles she had no one to share with.

She flipped lazily through a paper calendar she'd found in the study. The page still showed June 2024. Mid-month. The world's last normal week.

Rita didn't look up. She just waved her fingers in a sloppy half-sign, the kind that meant she wasn't really paying attention: Go on. Supply day.

Faith lifted her pillowcase from the table and gave a small nod. She waited for Rita to say something more, some reminder or instruction, but Rita was already absorbed in the calendar again, tracing dates that no longer meant anything.

Faith slipped into the mudroom and pulled on cracked boots by the door. The laces were mismatched, one frayed so badly it had to be tucked inside. She took her backpack off the wall and threw it over her shoulders and adjusted her straps, tightening them.

The mansion's front door was heavy, an old carved oak slab that complained in a low shaky rumble when she pushed it open. A blast of cold October air surged past her legs, sweeping dry leaves into the foyer behind her. They skittered across the marble like brittle insects, clicking faintly against the stone.

Faith stepped onto the wide front steps.

The world outside was quiet, stripped bare by the season. Brown leaves drifted over the driveway. The sky was a pale, washed-out blue. The neighborhood beyond the gate sat frozen in time, every house still paused in the summer of last year, but covered now by the slow crumble of nature reclaiming everything.

She pulled her sweater sleeves down over her hands, tightened her grip on the pillowcase, and took her first step down the long walkway.

Alone.

Faith followed the cracked sidewalk past the mansion's iron gate. The air bit at her cheeks, colder the farther she got from the mansion. Leaves scraped across the pavement in quick, jagged movements. She couldn't hear them, but she watched the dry flashes of color dart over the cracked asphalt like tiny creatures fleeing from her shadow.

She kept her eyes forward. She didn't count the houses anymore.

When they first arrived, Rita had sent her to the closest ones. The mansion's neighbors, an easy circle around the cul-de-sac. Then one street over. Then two. Then three. Every day, one house farther. One front lawn farther. One silent doorway farther.

Four months later, Faith had nearly reached the end of the neighborhood.

The homes here looked exactly like the ones closer in, just… more forgotten. This part of the neighborhood felt heavier. Untouched for longer.

Her boots pressed into patches of overgrown grass as she cut across a yard. A small bicycle lay beside a mailbox, its metal frame dulled with rust. The chain had fallen off and curled like a dead snake in the weeds. Faith paused, brushing her fingers over its handlebar. It had once been bright blue, she could still see the color fighting through the rust. It wobbled under her hand, but only felt cold.

Faith hugged her pillowcase closer against her chest and walked up the next driveway.

The front door of the house stood half-open, pushed by months of wind. She nudged it gently with her fingertips and stepped through the doorway. The air inside hung still, stale with the soft scent of old fruit. A bowl on the counter held shriveled apples and pears collapsing inward, their skins wrinkled like paper.

She moved carefully, as she always did, checking each drawer, then the pantry. A few cans. A box of crackers with a hole chewed in the corner. She took the cans and left the rest.

On the fridge, magnets held up schoolwork decorated with stickers. Essays with neat handwriting. A permission slip for a field trip to the zoo. A lunch menu for the week of June 10th. None of it got crossed off.

A backpack sat by the front door, straps folded neatly as if waiting for its owner to sling it on for one more Monday.

Faith stopped in the hallway, her breath catching when she saw the girl's bedroom.

The girl who lived here had been her age.

Maybe a little younger.

The bed was made with a sunflower blanket tucked neatly at the corners. A corkboard on the wall held track ribbons, bright even in the dusty light. A half-finished worksheet lay on the desk, pencil still placed across the lines where someone had paused mid-answer.

On the bed lay an open catalog.

Halloween costumes. Kids smiling with painted faces. Pirates, cats, witches, zombies. A page of glittery wings.

Faith reached out and touched the glossy corner.

Her fingertip stilled.

She pulled her hand away.

This should have been her October.

Dressing up for school…

Walking through hallways with friends…

Trading candy…

Planning costumes…

Instead, she was here.

In a stranger's house.

In stolen clothing.

With a pillowcase meant for canned soup instead of candy.

It was enough to pull tears to her eyes. Faith blinked hard and stepped away.

She went to the pantry, rummaging through boxes and bags until something small and crinkled slid into view. A fun-size candy bar tucked behind a stack of hardened oatmeal packets.

Her breath hitched.

She picked it up carefully, like it might break. The wrapper was cold and a little soft around the edges. She held it carefully, thumb running over the warped chocolate inside.

When she stepped back outside, the cold hit again. A light wind sweeping down the street, rustling dry leaves into spirals. Faith sat on the wooden porch steps, the boards shifting under her weight.

She opened the candy bar slowly. The chocolate had bloomed faintly white, but it melted on her tongue all the same. She let it dissolve, eyes tracking the swirl of leaves drifting across the yard.

She watched leaves fall across the lawn and tried to swallow the tightness in her chest.

I should be trick-or-treating, she thought.

She took another small bite, pressed her sleeve to her face, and swallowed hard.

When the candy was gone, she stood, brushed dried chocolate from her fingers, and walked toward the next house.

By the time Faith reached the mansion's long driveway, her arms ached from carrying the pillowcase. It wasn't heavy, just awkward, biting into the soft part of her palm. The late afternoon light had dimmed into a cold, washed-out gold, the kind that made the world look older than it was.

She pushed open the front door with her shoulder. The familiar heaviness rolled through her body as the oak slab shifted, and Faith stepped into the foyer.

Rita was waiting, as usual.

She stood in front of the tall, dust-streaked mirror, wrapped in a different fur coat. Pale gray this time, the collar oversized and dramatic. She held the edges like she was posing for an audience. The coat swallowed her shape, made her look softer than she was.

She didn't look up.

She just turned slightly, admiring her reflection.

Faith set the pillowcase down near the pantry. Rita didn't ask what she'd found. She just adjusted the coat again, shaking the sleeves out like she was preparing for a night out rather than a dead neighborhood.

Finally, Rita turned halfway toward her and moved her mouth slowly, casually, "Cold today, huh?"

Faith nodded once.

Rita looked out the window, arms folding around herself. Her eyes tracked the trees swaying outside, the early hints of frost on the grass. She shrugged, almost to herself. "Seasons don't really mean anything anymore." She said it with a little laugh, the brittle kind she used when she was trying too hard to sound unbothered.

Faith began unpacking the food. Two cans. A packet of noodles. A single fruit cup. Rita's eyes flicked over the items, and her shoulders tightened just barely, just enough to notice.

She pulled at a loose piece of fur on the coat's sleeve, avoiding Faith's eyes as she added, softer:

"Time doesn't matter without people."

She said it like she was repeating something she'd been thinking about for days.

Faith didn't answer. She placed the cans in the pantry, stacking them neatly.

Rita cleared her throat, an unnecessary gesture, but she did it anyway, and forced a smile, lifting the coat's collar dramatically.

"Someone owned this," her lips shaped. "Someone rich. Someone… probably annoying."

Her smile twitched, then faded.

Her voice dropped as she smoothed the front of the coat, almost a whisper Faith had to watch closely to understand:

"They'll come back eventually."

Faith stared at her.

A week ago, Rita had sworn people weren't coming back.

Two weeks ago, she said the world was theirs now.

Today… she wanted to impress ghosts.

Then, quickly, as if justifying herself, "We should make it nice for when they do."

Faith's stomach tightened.

She finished stacking the last can, wiped her hands on her sweater, and signed "You said people aren't coming back."

Rita's smile vanished.

Her eyes went flat, like shutters sliding down behind them.

She hugged the fur coat tighter around herself.

After a long pause, she muttered the words, small and tight "Well… maybe I was wrong."

Faith nodded once, more out of habit than agreement.

She folded the pillowcase and set it back on the table. The mansion felt colder than before, like the air had thinned around them.

Rita didn't look at her again.

Chapter 7

The sun was already sinking when Faith pedaled out of the last neighborhood, her cart tugging behind her like an extra heartbeat. The November air bit harder than October ever had. Thin and sharp, slicing through the spaces her scarves couldn't cover. She tugged the wool higher over her mouth, the edges stiff with cold, and blinked behind the fogged goggles.

The e-bike hummed under her, barely. The battery bar had been stuck at half since she'd found it, never rising, never dipping, like it had given up pretending to be useful. She pedaled to keep it moving, her thighs aching under the layers and weight.

Her cart was full enough: six cans of soup, a shoebox of matches, a cracked flashlight, a sweater she thought Rita might like but would probably critique anyway, a few stacks of cash, and a bag of gaudy jewelry. She'd pushed farther than she ever had today, past the manicured cul-de-sacs, past the rows of silent houses, past the first hint of commercial streets that bordered the old city edge.

She wanted to be home before the light fully drained from the sky, and if she pushed, she'd make it.

The wind coming off the pavement carried flecks of cold dirt and dry leaves. She felt them pepper her jeans and sting her knuckles through her mittens. The world looked colorless, all grays and deep shadows. The trees had given up most of their leaves already, only the pines bearing color. Branches stuck out like old bones against the pale sky.

The road here was wider. Straighter. No longer neighborhood-calm. It felt like a place where cars should be passing, even though they hadn't for months.

Faith leaned forward, urging the bike to keep its slow, stubborn pace.

The gas station came into view as she rounded the bend. A Sunoco, the kind with a half-size convenience store and six pumps under a faded blue canopy. The windows were dark. The space looked abandoned, like everything else, but less frozen. More unsettled. Something about it made her grip the handlebars tighter.

She hadn't been this far before.

The station sat at the edge of two worlds: the last stretch of quiet suburb and the start of a busier road leading toward the city. She stopped pedaling for a moment, letting the bike roll on its own.

Just a few more minutes and she'd be past it. Home wasn't far.

She told herself that twice.

Faith lowered her gaze to the cracked pavement passing beneath her tires... when something shifted in her peripheral vision.

Movement.

A shape behind the pumps.

Not a deer.

Not wind.

Not a trick of fading light.

A person. A real life actual person!

Faith's hands tightened on the grips until her knuckles hurt under her gloves. She slowed the bike to a stop without meaning to, her breath warming the inside of her scarf in fast, shallow bursts.

She blinked once, twice, trying to make sense of the figure stepping out from between the pump aisles.

Someone was there. Someone alive.

And he was smiling.

Faith coasted to a slow stop, one foot dragging lightly against the pavement as she tried to make sense of the man walking out from between the pumps. He moved like he'd been waiting there a long time. His hands shoved in his pockets, shoulders tight, a smile stretched wide across his face. The smile didn't look angry or threatening. It looked too happy. Too eager. Too practiced. Like seeing her wasn't a surprise but a wish he'd been holding onto.

He lifted a hand in a wave, but it came out stiff and uneven.

"Hey!" he called out. She saw the word shape clearly on his lips. "Hey, wait a second!"

Faith didn't answer. She tightened her grip on the handlebars and shook her head once, hoping that would be enough to make him stay back.

He took a step closer anyway.

"I'm not gonna hurt you," he said, exaggerating each word like he thought speaking slowly made him safer. "I just... I haven't seen anybody in months."

Faith raised one hand off the handlebar and signed carefully, I CAN'T HEAR YOU.

The man blinked. A small moment of confusion crossed his face.

Then a spark.

"Oh," he mouthed. "Ohhh, okay. Okay."

He tried to sign something back.

It was wrong.

Sloppy.

Something he must've remembered from a class he took once or a tutorial he half-watched.

Faith stayed still.

He smiled wider, trying again, hands making vague, clumsy shapes.

Not real signing, just an attempt to look understanding.

"See?" his mouth formed. "I get it. It's okay."

His motions didn't mean anything.

The man's expression flickered when she didn't react, but he forced another smile and reached into his jacket. He pulled out a crumpled protein bar and held it up like a peace offering. He tilted it side to side, nodding as if that would convince her. Then he gestured again, a simple curling of fingers. Come here.

Faith shook her head.

Then he held out the protein bar, nodding toward her like the offer should bridge every gap between them. He pointed to himself, then toward her. His mouth moved in a slow, careful rhythm, words shaped wide so she could read them. "You're safe." What he signed didn't match that at all.

Faith still didn't move.

He took a step forward.

Her grip tightened on the handlebars. She didn't pedal away. She didn't turn the bike around. She just shifted one foot, the smallest adjustment, and that was enough for him to decide she wasn't going to run.

He closed the distance fast.

Before she could react, his hand closed around her wrist. The grip wasn't painful at first, just firm. Steady in a way that made the hair rise on the back of her neck. He leaned in a little, his face softening, eyes searching hers with too much intensity.

"I haven't seen a person in so long," he mouthed.

Faith pulled her wrist back instinctively, but the pressure around it tightened. The protein bar slid from his hand, forgotten. His other hand came up from his side holding a wrench she hadn't seen before. He didn't swing it. He just showed it to her.

"Don't go," he mouthed, voice shaping the words slow and careful. "Don't. I'm alone. Don't go."

Faith shook her head hard, trying to yank her arm free. Her breath fogged the inside of her scarf in fast bursts. She signed with her free hand, messy and scared, "LET ME GO!"

The man's expression changed.

Whatever softness he'd been trying to project dropped out of his face.

He yanked her forward.

Hard.

Faith flew off the bike, her boot slipped on the pavement, and she fell sideways, hitting the ground on her shoulder. The shock of it rattled up her spine. She pushed to sit up, but he was already grabbing her again. This time by her upper arm dragging her backward across the concrete toward the road.

Her goggles knocked crooked across her face. Her scarf slipped down, cold air hitting her teeth. She kicked and twisted, trying to break free.

She screamed. She felt the air tear out of her chest.

But it didn't matter. He didn't stop.

He hauled her toward the center of the road, his breath visible in fast clouds, the wrench still clutched in his other hand. His mouth stretched open in a shout she couldn't hear, but she saw it clearly.

"THERE'S NO ONE TO HELP YOU, LITTLE GIRL!"

Faith's heart hammered against her ribs. She clawed at the pavement, boots scraping uselessly. Her glove ripped on broken asphalt. She tried to twist out of his grip, tried to dig her heels in, but he was stronger and desperate and pulling her with a kind of frantic purpose she didn't understand.

"You're gonna end up just like all of them," his mouth formed as he raised the wrench over his head. "Gone, just like everyone else!"

Then... something shifted under her.

A tremor.

Faint at first.

Running up through the surface of the road.

A familiar vibration. The same hum she'd felt that day in June.

Faith froze.

So did he.

The air pressure changed.

The cold thickened.

Her chest tightened like she'd stepped into a place too small for air.

A burst of bright light hit the pavement beside them.

Headlights.

Sharp.

White.

Closing fast.

They washed over her like a flash of midday sun, too sudden, too bright to make sense, too warm for the air outside. The vibration grew stronger, humming up her legs, humming in her bones. The man spun toward the light, eyes wide, face twisting in terror. The wrench slipped from his hand and clattered across the road. He dropped to his knees, arms thrown over his head, shielding himself from something that should have been there... What should have been barreling toward them...

But wasn't.

Faith curled into herself, instinctively bracing.

The headlights flared, and vanished.

The vibration stopped.

Silence.

No truck.

No engine.

No anything.

The man stayed crouched, shaking, staring into empty road.

Faith didn't wait for him to recover.

She scrambled to her feet, grabbed the bike with shaking hands, and dragged it across the pavement. The cart bounced wildly behind her, cans clattering. Her breath tore through her scarf in choked bursts. Her eyes blurred with tears she didn't remember starting.

She didn't look back.

She didn't care if he stood up.

She leapt onto the bike and hoped she had enough energy to get away.

She'd never pedaled so hard in her life.

Faith pedaled the bike up the long driveway, the cart dragging behind her in uneven jerks. Her arms shook from adrenaline and fear. The sky was fully dark now, no twilight left, just cold November air biting through her tear soaked scarf and the sting of her palms every time she gripped the handlebars tighter than she meant to.

Her face was stiff with dried tears. Her goggles were fogged at the edges. Her shoulder throbbed from the fall. Every breath came in short, fast bursts she couldn't slow.

The mansion's front windows glowed faintly, warm light spilling onto the porch. It felt wrong. Too normal. Too calm after what she'd just escaped.

Faith dragged the bike up the last few feet, let it tip against the railing, and stumbled the rest of the way inside.

Rita was in the foyer sorting through a pile of clothes she'd taken from one of the upstairs closets. Scarves. Gloves. A fur-lined vest she'd hung over a dining chair like she was building an outfit. She glanced up when Faith burst in, only a glance at first, then her eyes dropped straight to the cart outside.

Her mouth moved. "That's all you got?"

Faith stood shaking in the doorway, chest heaving. Her fingers stung as she lifted them to sign.

"THERE WAS A MAN. AT THE GAS STATION. HE GRABBED ME-"

Rita waved a hand sharply before Faith could finish.

"Slow down," her lips formed, annoyed, like Faith was making too much noise even in silence. "I can't follow when you're flailing everywhere."

Faith tried again. Slower. Her hands trembled with every movement.

"A man grabbed me- He dragged me- There was a truck. Lights. The ground shook- I thought I was going to die... Mom, I'm scared!"

Rita snorted, and shook her head in disbelief. She turned back to the pile of scavenged clothes, picking up a sweater and feeling the softness of the fabric like that mattered more than the story.

"Faith," her mouth shaped, "There was no man. No. You imagined it."

Faith stared at her. Her signing stalled midair. Rita wasn't going to believe her...

Rita kept going, irritation growing.

"There's nobody out there. We haven't seen anyone in four months." She held up a glove like she was checking it for holes. "You're worked up. Panicking. You probably got spooked by an animal or something."

Faith swallowed hard. Her hands tightened into fists before she opened her mouth. She took her time, patiently working the words out. "There was a man, Mom."

Rita shook her head again. Too fast. A flicker of something frantic behind her eyes.

"No. No." She jabbed a finger toward the door. "If someone was out there, we would've seen them by now."

Her lips tightened into a brittle, dismissive line. "There's nobody, Faith. Nobody. It's just us. You scared yourself."

Faith felt something sink inside her, low and heavy.

It wasn't just that Rita didn't believe her.

It was that Rita refused to even consider it, like the idea of someone else existing was more frightening than the alternative.

Rita sighed hard through her nose and pointed toward the cart again, as if remembering the important part.

"Please tell me you at least found more than a few cans."

Faith didn't answer.

She couldn't.

She stepped back from Rita slowly, her ribs aching with every breath. She wiped her scraped palms on her sweatpants, feeling grit stick to her skin, and went into the kitchen. The walls felt colder than outside.

She dug through the drawer by the fridge until she found a battered notebook. Brown cover, bent corners, half the pages wrinkled. She sat at the table, shoulders hunched, and opened to a blank page.

Her hand shook as she wrote.

Things I KNOW happened:

tremor under the road

pressure in the air

headlights too bright

no engine

no truck

the man was real

She pressed her palm flat to the floor beside her chair.

No vibration.

No hum.

Just cold tile and silence.

She picked up the pencil again and wrote the date in the corner.

She underlined the last word:

<u>REAL</u>.

Chapter 8

The morning cold hit harder now.

Not the sharp sting of October, or the creeping chill of early November. This was winter cold. The air was wet, heavy, and clinging to everything. The world outside the mansion looked washed out under a pale gray sky, the driveway still slick from last night's rain. Thin frost clung to the grass in stiff white patches, and the bare branches overhead held beads of ice that glinted like broken glass.

Faith tightened the scarf around her mouth as she pushed the bike out into the driveway. The metal frame was freezing against her gloves, and her breath fogged in front of her with every exhale. She wore more layers than ever: two sweaters, a coat too big in the shoulders, mismatched gloves, and socks doubled under her boots. The T-ball bat sat strapped along the side of the cart, metal gleaming dully where paint had chipped away.

Rita didn't bother seeing her out anymore. She barely looked up from the couch when Faith passed through the foyer, just flicked her fingers in a sloppy half-sign that meant nothing and mouthed, "Watch out for 'the man.'" Her smirk lasted only a second before she turned back toward the silent TV, raising the volume out of habit.

Faith didn't react. She just tucked her chin deeper into her scarf and shoved open the front door.

Outside, the cold swallowed her immediately.

She pedaled slowly down the long driveway, tires slipping on wet leaves matted to the pavement. The bike's battery bar hadn't budged, always stuck somewhere between one line and two like it couldn't make up its mind, but still gave her a boost. She pedaled hard anyway, because without her legs, she feared it wouldn't move at all.

The world felt farther away in winter.

As she reached the busted iron gate at the neighborhood entrance, she slowed. Two of the posts leaned at odd angles from when Rita had driven through them the day of the vanishing.

Faith rode past.

The houses she passed were older now, farther out, beyond the ones she'd already scavenged dry. Roofs dripped meltwater. Icicles clung to gutters even though snow hadn't come yet. Front lawns were stiff with frost, and the windows looked darker somehow, fogged with cold and months of stale air.

She stopped at the first house on her list. A small blue two-story with a collapsed mailbox and a plastic Santa still lying face-down in the yard from last year. Faith parked the bike at the curb, pulled the notebook from her backpack, and scribbled a quick line:

DEC 10 - 9 AM

cold / no tremor / quiet

It steadied her to write it down.

She shoved the notebook back into her bag and headed inside.

The house smelled like nothing, air too cold to hold any scent. Frost had crept along the edges of the living room windows; thin sheets of ice cracked under her boots as she moved. She checked the pantry, found a few cans, and slid them into her pillow case. Every step of the familiar routine felt heavier. Slower. Like winter itself was pulling at her sleeves.

She took one break. Just one.

In a half-finished bedroom, sitting on the floor between two bookcases, Faith opened a granola bar she'd kept for herself. She ate it slowly, savoring each bite even though it tasted stale. It was the only part of the day that felt like hers.

Ten minutes, maybe less.

Just enough to breathe.

When she was done, she stood, put her gloves back on, brushed crumbs off her coat, and kept moving.

By midday she'd covered a half dozen houses. By early afternoon she reached the last one on the street, loading the final cans into the cart. The sky had already dimmed to a deeper gray, the kind that meant the sun was on its way down. Winter days cut her time in half, and she felt every lost minute pressing at her shoulders.

She tightened the straps on the cart, checked the bat again, then swung her leg over the bike.

Her legs were tired. Her fingers numb. But she pedaled anyway, the world around her growing colder with every hour she stayed out. Rita had stopped caring if she came home every night while scavenging. "It's not like there's anyone out there... Just don't come back empty handed."

The house was warm in the wrong way when Faith came back, stale heat from the gas fireplace Rita kept running all day. It made the air thick and sour. Her boots squeaked on the marble as she wheeled the bike inside and unhooked her pillowcase.

Rita was exactly where Faith expected her: sprawled across the long velvet couch like she owned the place. One of the mansion's fur coats draped around her shoulders, a crystal glass in her hand. She'd filled it with cheap wine from a grocery bag Faith brought home two weeks ago, swirling it like she was sampling something expensive.

The TV was on, volume high even though it didn't matter. Rita watched it like there was sound coming out of it, laughing at parts Faith couldn't hear and Rita couldn't either.

"There you are," Rita mouthed lazily, barely glancing over. "Took long enough. Thought you'd be out another night."

Faith set the pillowcase down, pulling out cans one by one. Soup. Beans. A boxed dinner kit. Rita eyed the contents with an exaggerated sigh.

"That's it?" she asked, lips curling. "You were out all day. You gotta bring back more than this, sweetheart."

Faith signed carefully, "The houses are further away. It takes longer, and it's cold!"

Rita waved a dismissive hand. "Excuses," she said without looking. She plucked a cracker from a plate beside her and shoved it into her mouth. "People didn't take anything. They just… left. You're not checking hard enough."

Faith took out the last few items from the pillowcase. Rita didn't thank her. She only leaned forward, eyes sharpening for a moment.

"Next time, get wine," she mouthed. "Real wine. Not that box crap."

Faith froze for a breath, then signed, "I'm afraid of the stores, they're dangerous."

Rita didn't even watch her hands. She was staring past her, out the sliding glass door like she expected someone to walk up the steps.

"They're coming back," she said suddenly. "I mean, people. People are coming back. They have to. We should fix this place up before they do. Maybe paint the dining room. Or the hall. Something bright." She lifted her glass and took another long sip. "Or maybe nobody's coming back. Hard to say."

Faith waited. Rita wasn't talking to her anymore. She was talking at her.

"When they come back," Rita continued, "they'll want things nice. We can show them we kept it all together here. You and me. We did good."

Faith signed quietly, "Who?"

Rita blinked, annoyed she'd interrupted her own thoughts. "People," she mouthed, like it was obvious. "Adults. Neighbors. Families. Someone's gotta show up eventually."

She took another slow drink. Her attention drifted to a stack of junk she'd piled by the stairs. Fancy coats, silver platters, dusty books she'd taken from three different houses but never opened. Hoarded things. Random things. Things she insisted would "matter later."

Faith pulled the zipper on her backpack open just enough to see the edge of the notebook. She slid it farther down so Rita wouldn't notice.

Rita didn't ask where she was going. She didn't offer dinner. She didn't look at Faith again.

She was talking about plans, about repainting, about who she might invite over when everything went back to normal. Words spilling with no direction, no weight, no room for Faith inside them.

Faith watched her lips move.

And realized Rita wasn't talking about "them."

She wasn't even talking about "both of us."

She was talking about herself.

And Faith wasn't part of that future at all. She wondered if she ever had been.

Faith spent as much time as she could in her room, away from Rita. Her room was colder than the hallway. The mansion never held heat right, too many tall windows, too much empty space, air slipping through places she couldn't see. She sat on her bed with the blanket wrapped around her shoulders, flashlight dim under the covers as she opened her notebook.

Her fingers were stiff from the day. She rubbed warmth into them and flipped back through entries she'd written and others she tried to remember.

June.

August.

October.

The tremors.

The phantom truck.

The days she'd doubted herself.

The nights she'd convinced herself she imagined it.

She wrote slowly:

December 10 - night

cold / quiet / no tremor yet

The words steadied her.

She held the pencil poised to keep writing, but stopped.

There it was again.

A faint vibration under the floorboards. Small. Barely there. Like the house was breathing differently, deeper, from somewhere beneath her room. It wasn't loud. It wasn't shaking anything. It was just a presence. A warmth under the wood that made her press her hand to the floor carefully, like she didn't want to scare it away. The warmth reminded her of Geno.

The hum pulsed once.

Then again.

Slow.

Rhythmic.

Her father used to walk heavy in their old house. She'd feel him before she saw him, boots on the stairs, the way he'd knock on the wall down the hallway so she could feel the small vibration through her mattress when he passed. She'd known his vibrations better than anyone, even before she learned how to read lips. She'd always felt safe when he was near.

For a moment, with her palm on the cold wood, the memory folded over the present.

Warm.

Surreal.

Almost believable.

She closed her eyes.

Not believing it was Geno, but wanting it to be.

The hum faded slowly, settling back into the boards until she wasn't sure if it had stopped… or if it had never really been there.

Faith lifted her head and took a breath.

She wrote a new line:

another tremor

stronger this time

The pencil lingered.

Her hand didn't move.

Then she wrote, "Dad?"

From down the hallway, Rita shouted something, Faith could feel the faint vibration in the walls from her voice. Her words slurred, irritated, muffled through walls. Faith flinched out of instinct. She snapped the notebook shut and slid it deep into her backpack, tucking the blanket around it until she couldn't see the edges.

She lay back on the mattress without taking off her boots. The cold in the corners of the ceiling spread in slow silver edges. The room felt too big around her.

She pressed her palm to the floor again.

Nothing now.

Just cold wood.

Just emptiness.

Faith stared at the ceiling.

She didn't even move.

Just a single quiet thought, heavy and steady, "I can't trust her anymore."

Another followed, softer, "I need to take care of myself."

She closed her eyes, blanket pulled tight, boots still on, the hum still ghosting her memory.

Not gone.

Not real.

Somewhere in between.

The house settled.

Faith did not.

Chapter 9

Faith reached the strip mall as the sun was already sliding behind the tree line, pulling the temperature down with it. The cold wasn't as sharp today. Still biting, still miserable, but not the kind that stabbed through her layers. Winter light didn't last long anymore. One minute it was afternoon, the next everything looked washed in a dull blue shadow. Her breath was hot and thick inside her scarf as she coasted to a stop in front of the old pharmacy.

The pharmacy sat at the far end of the plaza, lights long dead, windows fogged from months of cold. A sedan had crashed straight through the front doors. It still sat half inside, half out, its hood buried in a collapsed shelf. The impact must've happened the moment everything ended. No driver. No blood. Just frozen chaos.

She hesitated at the bike rack, weighing the shortcut home against the longer, safer route she took when she stayed out overnight. The sky was already dimming. She checked the bat strapped along her cart, fingers brushing the metal like a reminder.

It was already late. She should head home. Just in case.

Then she made her choice.

Rita wouldn't care.

And Faith wasn't ready to go back yet.

Inside, the pharmacy didn't look looted at all.

It looked like life had just... paused.

Shopping baskets sat half-filled on the floor, items still neatly arranged inside them. A wallet lay open on the front counter, bills folded halfway out like someone had been mid-payment. A prescription bag sat by the register with a pen resting across it. Displays stood untouched, dust settling on their glossy corners.

It was all too normal, too held-in-place.

The car crash was the only sign something had gone wrong.

Even the clocks on the wall were frozen with the time it happened. 8:03.

Faith stepped carefully between two aisles, boots sliding over coupon flyers that had curled with age. The emptiness here felt heavier than in the neighborhoods, like the store still expected its owners to come back from a lunch break.

She moved toward the back where first-aid supplies used to be stocked, her shoulders tight, bat gripped in both hands.

That's when she felt it... Just enough to stop her mid-step.

A faint vibration through the soles of her boots.

A shift of weight somewhere.

Not enough to tell what caused it.

Her fingers tightened around the bat. Faith raised the bat, breath hitching as she rounded the end of the aisle.

And there she was.

A woman knelt on the tile, organizing gauze and medical wraps into a plastic basket. Not hurried. Not frantic. Just working, like she'd slipped into routine because it kept her sane. She was in her late fifties, hair gone mostly gray, bundled in layers that looked scavenged but cared for. Her posture wasn't tense. She looked calm.

The woman turned, startled but not panicked. She lifted both hands immediately, palms out, showing she had nothing to grab. Nothing to hide.

She mouthed the words "It's okay."

Faith quickly motioned with her free hand, "I can't hear you."

The older woman smiled gently, her hands lowering before signing, gentle and fluent, "Are you okay? I won't hurt you."

Her motions were smooth. Confident. The kind of fluent hands Faith hadn't seen since the world was normal.

Faith didn't lower the bat, not all the way, but her grip loosened. She signed back, small and cautious, "I'm fine. Who are you?"

The woman's expression softened immediately. She didn't stand. She didn't move closer. She kept her distance, sitting back on her heels like she wanted Faith to see every choice she made.

Faith stayed at the end of the aisle, half-hidden behind a shelf. The woman nodded once in understanding and signed again, "It's okay. Take your time. My name is Mary."

Faith watched her for a long moment, waiting for the sudden shift, the change in expression she'd learned to fear. But it didn't come. The woman just waited, hands still, eyes steady, offering nothing but patience.

For the first time in months, Faith felt something inside her loosen. Not trust. Not yet.

Relief.

A tiny bit.

But real.

Mary led Faith toward the back of the pharmacy, weaving between tipped shelves and abandoned carts. They reached a small break area near the stockroom, where Mary had dragged an old propane heater into the center of the floor. A dented metal dish sat on top, steam drifting from a little pool of water mixed with curled orange peels. The scent was faint but soft, warm citrus cutting through the sterile cold of the store.

Mary flicked the ignition. The heater crackled to life, orange coils glowing slowly. Faith sank closer, holding her hands toward the warmth until the sting left her fingers.

Mary dug into her basket and pulled out a can of peaches. She handed it over with a tiny smile, then held up a fork and a questioning look. Faith nodded.

They ate slowly. The peaches were cold, but sweet. Softer than she expected. Faith took each bite carefully, savoring it, letting the syrup sit on her tongue before swallowing. She hadn't tasted anything like this in months. For a moment, she forgot about the bike outside, the cold night, Rita, everything.

Mary watched her with gentle eyes. Not pitying, just seeing her. Really seeing her.

After a few minutes, Mary reached into her coat pocket and pulled out a small notepad and a short pencil. She set them between them, tapping it lightly with one finger before sliding it toward Faith.

Faith hesitated.

Then wrote:

How long have you been here?

Mary read it, then wrote beneath it in looping, steady handwriting:

Since summer.

You?

Faith added:

June.

I was with someone but… it's not good now.

I wish my father was still here.

Mary nodded, expression softening. She signed carefully:

I had a son your age.

Faith's chest tightened. She didn't ask what happened. Mary didn't add anything else. Instead, Mary scribbled gently on the notepad:

I'm sorry.

You're very brave.

Faith's throat burned for a moment. She swallowed and wrote:

I'm not brave. I'm just trying to live.

Mary rested her hand lightly on Faith's shoulder, then removed it just as gently, letting Faith decide whether the contact stayed. It was the first human touch Faith hadn't recoiled from in months.

Mary signed:

Your ASL is beautiful.

I haven't seen another Deaf person yet.

I'm glad you made it.

Faith didn't know what to say. She looked down at her hands, then wrote:

You sign better than most hearing people.

Mary chuckled silently, covering her mouth, shoulders shaking. Her smile was warm and real. The kind that pushed lines into the corners of her eyes.

She took the notepad again and wrote:

There's a safe place near the mall.

A few of us gather supplies.

You can come with me if you want.

Faith froze. The idea hit her like a breath she hadn't expected. Someone else. Multiple someone else's. A safe place. Somewhere that wasn't Rita's cracked version of reality.

She didn't answer. Couldn't yet.

Mary didn't push. She just wrote:

No pressure.

Just don't do this alone if you don't have to.

They passed the notepad back and forth until the heater dimmed to a low orange glow. The store grew darker, sharper at the edges, but the little circle of light around them stayed warm.

For the first time in months, Faith smiled. Not the forced kind she gave Rita sometimes to avoid anger. A small, real smile that tugged gently at her cheeks.

Mary saw it and smiled back.

Eventually, Faith's head dipped forward, sleep pulling at her in slow waves. She curled up beside the heater, blanket around her shoulders, bat resting within reach. The warmth hummed softly through her bones, steady and safe.

Mary stayed awake a while longer, keeping watch.

Faith slept.

For one night, she wasn't afraid.

Faith woke before the sun.

At first she didn't know why, just that something felt different. Colder. She blinked in the dim blue light and pushed herself up on her elbows.

The heater was dark.

Out of fuel.

Barely warm at the edges.

And Mary's blanket was folded neatly beside it.

Faith's heart lurched. She turned quickly, scanning the break area, expecting Mary to be crouched behind a shelf or packing her basket again.

But the space was still.

No struggle.

No sign of panic.

No sound except the groan of winter wind slipping through the broken front doorway.

Just absence.

Faith stood shakily, blanket slipping off her shoulders, and looked around again. Once, then twice, then a third time, as if Mary might appear between blinks.

She didn't.

Something caught Faith's eye on the floor. A small can of peaches, placed carefully beside her backpack. And tucked underneath it, a folded piece of paper.

Her hands trembled as she picked it up.

The handwriting was the same looping, steady script from last night.

"Keep flying, little bird."

Faith read it once.

Then again.

Her throat tightened hard, like something inside her had been pulled too fast. She sat down on the cold tile before her legs gave out. The heater's metal casing was cold beneath her palm.

She held the note against her chest and cried.

Not the quiet leaking she'd done alone in bathrooms or under blankets. Not the controlled tears she swallowed back before Rita could see.

She sobbed.

Hard, shaking sobs she couldn't control, the kind that made her shoulders curl inward and her breath break in quick, painful hitches. She pressed her face into her sleeve, but the noises still came through. Raw and sharp, months of fear and loneliness and held-together silence unraveling all at once.

She cried because Mary was gone.

Because kindness had found her for one night and slipped away before she woke.

Because she hadn't realized how badly she needed it until she lost it.

Because people were still here.

When the crying finally slowed, she wiped her face with her sleeve, breath still hitching. She opened her backpack, pulled out her notebook, and slid the note inside the front cover.

She wrote under it in small, shaky letters:

proof that kindness exists

proof someone cared

proof that not everyone is like the man

proof that not everyone is Rita

proof I'm not alone

She underlined "I'm not alone" twice.

She closed the notebook softly, zipping it into the safest pocket she had.

Then she stood, pulling her scarf up around her red cheeks. She gathered her things slowly, quietly. Her blanket, the metal bat, the last can of peaches, and walked toward the broken front of the store.

Cold air hit her the moment she stepped outside. Sharp and biting against her skin, the kind of cold that carried straight through coat and bone.

But something about it didn't feel as empty today. She touched the outline of the pocket watch through her coat, her father's picture inside, and held it there for a moment longer than she needed to.

She tightened her scarf, gripped the handlebars of her bike, and began the long ride home.

For the first time since June, she didn't feel completely alone.

Chapter 10

Faith pedaled the last stretch of the driveway with legs that felt like rubber. Afternoon light barely clung to the sky; the sun was already sliding behind the mansion's tall roofline. Everything had that blue-gray quiet that came before winter evenings, the kind that felt more like night than day.

But she wasn't scared this time.

Her chest still held a little warmth from last night. From Mary, from the fire, from the soft way someone finally looked at her without irritation or need. It wasn't hope exactly, but it was something in that direction.

She pushed the bike up the final bit of driveway, breath fogging out in small bursts. The cart behind her was heavier than usual. Filled with extra bandages, vitamins, two bottles of pain meds, canned peaches, two bottles of wine, rubbing alcohol, cough drops, and a whole box of those cheap plastic lighters that everyone kept by their registers.

The mansion looked dead from the outside. No lights. No smoke from the chimney. No movement behind the windows.

Faith braced herself and went in.

The foyer was cold. The fireplace was off. Rita wasn't on the couch or in the kitchen. The air smelled stale from a whole day with no heat.

Faith dragged the bike inside and unhooked the cart, setting everything gently on the kitchen table. She began sorting quietly, medical supplies into one drawer, canned goods onto the pantry shelf, the lighters into the top drawer by the stove. She worked fast, efficient, hoping to finish before Rita wandered down in whatever mood she'd woken up in.

She had just crouched at the pantry, sliding a box of gauze into place, when a small tremor rolled through the ceiling above her, just enough to make her freeze. Faith stood slowly, turning. She looked around but saw nothing. Just as she started to drop back down to the pantry, motion caught in her peripheral.

Suddenly, a winded Rita stood at the bottom of the staircase, wild-eyed, hair matted from sleep, still wearing the same sweater from last night. She clutched an umbrella in one hand and a tennis racket in the other.

For a full second she looked like someone feral.

Then her face snapped into a dramatic mask of outrage.

"Where the HELL were you?" she mouthed, jabbing the umbrella toward her like a spear. "I was worried sick!"

Faith just stared at her. They both knew she'd been passed out all day. Faith raised her hands slowly, signing a small apology, nothing elaborate, just "I'm sorry, I worked late."

Rita didn't even look at the signs.

She stomped across the foyer into the kitchen, then tossed the tennis racket onto a chair like she suddenly didn't need it. "Do you have ANY idea what could've happened to you? Jesus, Faith. You can't just disappear for a whole night and-"

Her eyes landed on the cart's contents. The fake concern vanished so fast it left a hollow behind it. She reached past Faith, grabbed one of the wine bottles, and held it up to the light. "I guess this'll do," she mouthed, unimpressed.

She tucked it under her arm and walked off toward the kitchen without another glance, muttering to herself, already unscrewing the cap.

Faith stayed in the pantry doorway, hands still half-raised from the apology that went unseen. She swallowed, lowered them, and kept putting things away.

Behind her, cabinets slammed. Rita's footsteps grew fainter. The umbrella rolled across the tile until it hit the wall with a soft thud.

Faith stacked the last can of peaches on the shelf, tucked her scarf into her coat, and closed the pantry door gently so it wouldn't make a sound.

Dinner took longer than it should have.

The rice didn't want to soften in the cold kitchen. The canned soup hissed when she opened it, metal stiff from the winter air. Faith moved mechanically, layering cans into a pot, stirring slowly, wiping her hands on a towel she had to rinse twice because everything felt sticky.

Rita didn't come in to help once.

She was in the living room by the gas fireplace, wrapped in a fur coat like a throne blanket, wine already half gone. Faith could see the glow of the TV through the doorway as she set bowls on the table. Rita watching some DVD with the volume so loud Faith could feel it in the kitchen and the subtitles off so she couldn't enjoy it too.

When everything was ready, Faith carried the pot of soup to the table, then went to the living room doorway and signed to Rita, "Mom, dinner's ready."

Rita dragged herself up with a dramatic sigh, wine glass dangling in her hand. She plopped into her chair at the head of the table like she was arriving late to a banquet she'd hosted.

"You were gone all night," she mouthed, stabbing a spoon into her bowl before it even settled. "Do you know how that made me feel?"

Faith sat quietly across from her, hands resting in her lap. She signed carefully, slow enough for Rita to read without thinking, "I had to stay somewhere safe."

Rita scoffed loud enough Faith felt the vibration through the table. "Oh, safe?" she exaggerated with her lips, lifting her glass to point at the air. "Safe out there? So home isn't safe now, is that what you're saying?"

Faith looked down at her bowl, steam drifting upward. Her fingers moved again, smaller this time, "I'm sorry. But there was someone that-"

Rita rolled her eyes so hard her whole head moved. "Oh, for God's sake. Don't start with your stories. Not another imaginary man!"

Faith swallowed, then tried again. She signed, "I felt the hum again. Like my dad-"

Rita went still. Completely still.

Then burst into a laugh so loud Faith felt it in the floorboards.

"Your Father?" she mouthed, leaning forward like she needed to see Faith's face up close. "Don't start with that pretend crap again."

Faith's chest tightened. She shook her head, fumbling her signs slightly in the urgency, "I can show you. Just look here!"

She reached for her backpack, pulled out her notebook, flipping quickly through pages she'd written late at night under blanket light.

She turned it toward Rita.

Rita didn't even glance. She waved a hand like shooing a fruit fly.

"None of this even makes sense," she mouthed. "Your father? He wasn't even there for you when he was alive. And now the whole world's gone and you think he's alive?"

Faith's throat tightened like it wanted to close entirely.

Rita leaned in, wine breath drifting over the table. "You're so fucking stupid sometimes," her lips formed, slow and cruel. "Such a naïve little girl. You wouldn't last ten minutes out there without me."

Faith reached for her notebook, slow and trembling.

But Rita beat her to it.

She set her wine glass down directly on top of it, just a touch too fast, deliberate enough that wine sloshed over the rim and bled into the cover.

"Whoops," she mouthed, without an ounce of apology. "I think I'll keep this for now. We've heard enough of your little stories."

She took one more lazy drink, grabbed the notebook, stood, and walked away toward the fireplace, already reaching for the fresh bottle of wine she'd pulled from the cart earlier.

"Clean up this mess," she tossed over her shoulder, not bothering to turn.

Faith stayed at the table, staring at the spreading wine stain, hands motionless in her lap, breath barely moving in her chest, teeth clenched.

The room pressed in around her, heavy and silent.

The house felt bigger after Rita left the dining room.

Not quieter. Just empty in a way Faith could feel in her ribs.

Rita shuffled off toward the living room, the fur coat dragging behind her like a shed skin. She wrapped it tighter around her shoulders, grabbed her wine by the neck, and collapsed onto the couch. She didn't even bother turning the volume down. The TV flashed bright colors over her face while a DVD menu looped endlessly, sound blasting into the room for no one's benefit.

She stared at it like it meant something. Like she wasn't the reason everything felt wrong.

Faith stayed at the table long after Rita was gone.

She washed the dishes alone. Scrubbed the pot twice. Cleaned the spilled wine off the table with a rag she rinsed until her hands burned with cold. Every soundless clatter of ceramic against ceramic felt bigger inside her chest than anything coming from the TV.

She dried her hands on her sleeves and stood still, staring down the hall. Her mind spun webs of wild thought.

Left, the door. Freedom. She could run away and try to make it on her own.

Straight, the fireplace where Rita swayed in her blanket, bottle tipped to her lips, eyes glassy.

Right, the stairs leading up to her bedroom. She could at least hide from herself up there.

Faith stayed at the table long after the dishes were dry, hands pressed flat against the wood as if hoping for some sign from her father. The room stretched quiet around her, the mansion wide and cold and too big for two people who didn't know how to be family.

She looked toward the living room. Rita sat slumped by the fire, wine glass dangling from her fingers, the TV flashing colors she wasn't even watching. She wasn't worried. She wasn't angry. She wasn't anything Faith needed her to be.

Faith swallowed hard and finally pushed herself to stand. She let a slow breath out.

She turned toward the staircase and started up, each step careful, measured, the house creaking under her weight like it wanted to hold her back.

At the top of the stairs, she paused to let the quiet settle around her like something she could finally hear. Something honest.

Then she walked into her room and closed the door softly behind her.

Chapter 11

The house was colder than it should have been.

Faith lay awake for a long time, staring at the ceiling, listening to nothing. Her breath made little clouds with each tiny exhale. The fireplace downstairs must've died out hours ago; the air pressed icy against her face.

Her stomach hurt.

She hadn't finished dinner.

She hadn't really eaten at all.

She waited until she was sure Rita wouldn't come upstairs. Then she slid out of bed, boots in hand, and padded barefoot down the hall. The floorboards were cold enough to sting, but she was afraid to make any sound Rita may hear.

At the bottom of the stairs, she paused, peering into the living room. Rita was passed out sideways in the fur coat, one arm hanging off the couch, empty wine glass still clutched in her fingers. The TV screen glowed blue against her face, the same DVD menu looping, subtitles off, volume a physical pressure even Faith could feel in her ribs.

Faith held her breath and moved toward the kitchen.

She opened the pantry slowly, fingertips careful on the edge of the door. Everything inside was still and dim. She scanned the shelves, reached for one of the cans of peaches she'd hidden behind the stacked soups, and cradled it against her chest like it might make noise.

She grabbed a spoon from the drawer and sat at the edge of the dining table, as far from the living room as she could get. Her bare toes curled against the cold tile.

She popped the can open with a soft metallic click, trying her best to do it as slowly and soundlessly as possible.

The scent of syrup drifted up. Warm memories, warm safety, warm Mary.

Faith swallowed once and began to eat, small bites, slow and quiet.

Spoon tapping gently against aluminum.

Heart beating even faster.

She didn't want trouble.

She just wanted to stop shaking inside.

Faith had only taken a few bites when Rita's shape lurched into the doorway.

A blanket hung crooked off her shoulders like shedding fur. Her hair stuck out in tangled clumps, mascara smudged below her eyes, wine glass gripped so tightly her knuckles had gone pale. She swayed once, caught herself on the doorframe, then blinked hard like the room offended her by existing.

Her gaze slid to the table. To the can of peaches.

To Faith.

The rage hit instantly. She threw the glass across the kitchen, sending shards across the floor. Rita's lips pulled back, ugly and sharp. "You think you deserve those?" she mouthed, each word big and sloppy, spit shining on her lip.

Faith froze halfway through lifting the spoon.

Rita staggered forward, pointing with the glass. "Ungrateful little girl," her mouth snapped. "Sneaking around. Eating like you earned anything."

Faith set the spoon down slowly, fingers trembling.

Rita didn't stop.

"Your imaginary man?" she mouthed, mocking the shape of each syllable. "Your stupid little notebook? You think that means something? You think you did something worth eating?"

Before Faith could react, Rita lunged.

Her hand swung out, smacked the can from Faith's grip. Peaches flew, syrup spattering across the table and dripping onto the tiles below.

Faith gasped silently, scooting back in her chair. She lifted her hands in small, placating signs. "I'm sorry, Mom. I'll stop. I didn't mean-"

Rita cut her off by flapping her own hands back at her in a warped, exaggerated mockery of signing. Her fingers jerking wildly, tongue poking from the corner of her mouth, face twisted in a cruel imitation.

Then she laughed. Loud enough that Faith felt it through the chair legs. "How many times have I told you to use your fucking words!" Her hand struck out and slapped Faith's down.

"You don't mean anything," Rita mouthed, stepping closer, the sour heat of wine rolling off her breath. "Not to me. Not to your dead worthless father. You think you're the victim here? You think you're special?"

Faith shook her head quickly, hands up, backing away from the table.

Rita followed. Stumbling but relentless. The room seemed to shrink around them.

The heat rose in Faith's cheeks. Something ugly was ready to blow.

Faith took a step back from the table, palms raised, trying to keep the situation from boiling over. Her feet slipped in the sticky peach juice that had spilled from where Rita had slapped them, syrup glistening on the tile. Broken glass lay scattered near Rita's feet from the wine she'd thrown earlier, and Faith stepped carefully around it as she moved toward the stairs. Her heart was thumping hard now, the kind that made her chest feel too small.

She didn't want this. She didn't want any of it.

Rita staggered after her, blanket half-dragging along the floor, one hand against the wall to steady herself. Her eyes were unfocused, but her mouth never stopped moving. Angry, sloppy, cruel shapes full of blame Faith couldn't hear but understood anyway.

"Broken," she mouthed, pushing off the wall and lurching closer. "Worthless. Good for nothing."

Faith shook her head and signed small, frightened motions, nothing combative, just an attempt to slow things down. She tried to step sideways, tried to slip past Rita's reach and make it up the stairs to her room where she could shut the door and breathe.

But Rita moved faster than she should've, stumbling right into the space between Faith and the stairs. She jabbed a finger toward Faith's chest, her lips twisting as she mouthed something sharp, "I'll make sure you can hear me!"

The shove came out of nowhere.

Hard, clumsy, fueled by wine and frustration, her hand slamming into Faith's shoulder. Faith's body jolted backward. Instinct took over, pure reflex, and she shoved back.

Rita was too drunk to absorb it.

She stumbled once, arms flailing loosely. Her slipper caught the edge of the rug. Her hip twisted the wrong way. For half a second her eyes went wide, not from anger but from surprise. Real, sober surprise.

Then she dropped.

Her head struck the bottom stair with a dull, sickening crack.

And everything went white.

Faith froze, hand still half-raised, breath clamped in her throat. She didn't move.

Couldn't.

Her fingers trembled as she stepped around a shard of glass and knelt beside her mother, reaching out with shaking hands. She hovered there, terrified to touch her, terrified not to.

"Mom?" she mouthed, forcing sound out with it.

Rita didn't answer.

She didn't even twitch.

Faith's breath hitched, panic rising fast and hot behind her ribs. She lowered herself beside Rita, knees hitting the cold tile, and reached out again, this time laying a hand on Rita's shoulder, hoping for any response at all.

"Mom, wake up!"

Nothing.

Faith stared at her mother's stillness, guilt twisting hard through her stomach as the truth hit her in waves. She might have killed her. She might actually be alone now. Completely alone.

For a long time, Faith didn't move.

She stayed kneeling beside Rita, staring at her mother's unmoving chest, waiting for something to rise, fall, twitch...

Anything.

Her own breath came shallow. Her hands hovered uselessly in the air before dropping to her sides. Minutes passed. Maybe two. Maybe twenty. The house felt suspended. Like time itself forgot to check on her.

When she finally pushed herself upright, her legs trembled. Not from shock, though there was that, but from the strange, hollow calm sitting in her chest. She expected tears. Expected some kind of collapse. But nothing came. Just a soft, numb ache, the kind that didn't feel real yet.

She looked down at Rita again.

Her mother didn't stir.

Faith let out one shaky exhale through her nose. She didn't want to stay. Not here. Not after this. Not with the fear sitting in her ribcage like a brick.

She moved like she was wading through deep water.

First, her backpack. She found it by the dining table, strap tangled, zipper half open where Rita had rifled through it earlier. Faith lifted the wine glass from her notebook, sticky from the spill, and slid the notebook inside the bag before Rita could ever touch it again.

Her coat came next. She shrugged into it slowly, arms stiff, scarf wrapped around her neck with careful motions, gloves tugged on one finger at a time. She didn't want sound. Didn't want to disturb whatever stillness the house was holding.

She dug into the pocket of the jacket, deep through the little hole, and felt it. Still safely tucked inside. Faith cupped the pocket watch with her fathers picture in her hand, thumb gliding across the dent on its surface, then tucked it back through the hole to safety.

Her eyes drifted to the kitchen. There, she grabbed two cans, one soup, one peaches, and slipped them into her bag. Not much, but enough for a day or two. She didn't think she'd be gone long. She didn't know. She didn't have a plan beyond leaving. Maybe she could search for Mary. Or her father.

Before she left the kitchen, she reached for her bat where it leaned against the cart. Her fingers gripped the cold metal automatically.

Faith walked back to the stairs. Rita still hadn't moved.

Faith stood there for a moment, looking at her mother's still form, wondering why her chest didn't feel cracked open. Wondering why she wasn't sobbing on the floor. Wondering if something was wrong with her, or if something had broken way earlier than tonight.

She reached one hand out, barely, fingers twitching toward her mother. Then she pulled it back.

She turned toward the front door, backpack on, watch in pocket, bat in hand.

She wasn't going to look back.

Faith had one hand on the doorknob.

Just one.

The house was so still she could feel her own pulse in her teeth. She pulled the door open an inch, just enough to slip through, when something behind her shifted. Something she felt: a change in the air. The weight of another person's breath entering the space.

She froze. Turned.

Rita was standing at the bottom of the stairs.

Awake. Steady on her feet. No wobble, no confusion. Just a sharp, glassy alertness that made her look older and crueler in the cold hallway light. Blood matted her hair where she'd hit the step, but she didn't touch it. Didn't acknowledge it. Her eyes were locked on Faith with a clarity that made Faith's stomach drop.

"Go."

No slurring now.

No drunken sway.

Just something hollow and calculated.

"Go ahead. Get out!"

Rita's mouth curled into a slow, humorless smile.

"You think you can live without me?" she mouthed, each word shaped with cutting precision.

Faith didn't move.

Rita stepped closer, barefoot on the tile, movements too controlled for someone who'd been unconscious seconds ago.

"Get!" she mouthed. "Go on. Since you know everything. Since you're so grown."

Faith tried to tighten her grip on the backpack strap, but Rita was already reaching for it.

"I'm tired of taking care of a broken child."

She yanked the strap hard, ripping it out of Faith's hands. Faith stumbled forward, catching herself on the doorframe.

Rita pulled the front door wide open and, with one sharp swing, hurled the backpack into the driveway. It skidded across the concrete, spilling a can that rolled until it hit the garden border.

Rita looked right at her.

"Let's see how far your ghosts get you."

Faith felt her fingertips go numb. Rita leaned in close enough that Faith could see the drying wine stain on her chin.

"Maybe your father will answer back this time." She straightened, slammed the door shut between them, and locked the deadbolt without hesitation.

Faith stood on the porch, the cold biting through her layers, snow beginning to drift sideways in thin, icy flakes. Behind her, the mansion glowed warm through the windows, gold, distant, and something she could see but no longer belonged to.

She didn't knock.

She didn't cry.

She stepped off the porch, walked into the driveway, picked up her backpack, and pulled the strap over her shoulder with shaking hands. She turned, picking up the can by the garden. She pulled her e-bike from beside the trash cans.

Then she turned toward the empty road.

Toward the mall.

Toward Mary's "safe place."

Toward anything that wasn't this.

And she left.

Act 3

My world was born quiet...
But even the silence here...
Is deafening.

Chapter 12

Faith woke with her cheek pressed to hardwood and the cold already inside her bones. She started growing used to that feeling.

For a minute she didn't move. Didn't even open her eyes. She just lay there with her breath making thin little clouds above the floorboards, each one dissolving faster than the last. Her joints ached before she stretched them; her knuckles felt swollen, cracked, rough from weeks of dry wind and cheap gloves.

The fire had gone out hours ago. Only a faint curl of ash sat in the brick mouth of the fireplace, a ghost of the warmth she'd borrowed from it. It was the only smell in the cold that was strong enough to cut through.

She opened her eyes.

The living room around her still carried the shape of a party. Streamers hung half-torn from the curtain rods. Paper cups lay scattered across the carpet, the kind with cartoon balloons printed on them. A plate of cupcakes was frozen together on the coffee table, their icing stiff and collapsed like tiny frosted gravestones. The banner, HAPPY BIRTHDAY, drooped in the middle, hung like it couldn't keep pretending anymore.

She pushed herself up slowly, coat stiff around her shoulders, backpack still wedged under her head the way she'd used it for a pillow. Her bat lay across her legs where she'd fallen asleep gripping it. She flexed her fingers around the handle again, wincing at the sting in her skin as the scabs pulled.

The house itself didn't look ransacked. She'd had to slip in through a basement window she cracked open with her boot heel, but the place was otherwise untouched. No footprints but hers. No signs of forced entry. No strangers hiding in hallways. It was safe enough for one night.

Safe enough to sleep without her heart in her throat.

She reached into her coat and pulled out the pocket watch. Her father's face stared back at her from behind the scratched glass, steady and soft. She brushed her thumb over the dent she always touched first, then she pressed her palm flat to the floorboards.

Nothing.

No hum.

No vibration.

Just cold wood and the faint creak of the house settling under winter.

She swallowed, throat tight and dry. She hadn't spoken since that night seven weeks ago with Rita. Her voice seemed like something someone else used to have.

Faith strapped on her backpack, adjusting the weight until it sat right against her shoulders. Just enough supplies for a day or two. She'd learned to trust untouched houses, not the burden of carrying everything with her. She slid the bat through the loop she'd added to the side strap, then pulled her gloves over her aching fingers one at a time.

The living room looked even colder now that she was standing in it.

Streamers swayed slightly in a draft from a window that was still cracked open. A plastic birthday hat lay half-crushed near the couch. She stepped over it and moved toward the front door.

Outside, the sky was pale and washed out. Snow drifted across the empty yard like dust. Faith tightened her coat around her and took her first breath of the morning air. It stung her ribs on the way in.

Then she stepped off the porch and into the winter, heading south without thinking.

It was where the hum always pointed her.

And it was the only thing she still trusted in this world.

Faith walked with her backpack pulled tight against her shoulders, boots crunching through the thin crust of snow lining Naaman's Road. The world here felt stretched and empty, the kind of quiet that didn't echo. Her breath drifted in front of her in pale wisps, disappearing before she could finish watching them.

Most days had blurred like this. Gray sky, cold air, and the numb rhythm of walking.

She'd abandoned the e-bike weeks ago. She still remembered pushing it through slush, watching the battery die, the back tire crack, the chain snap during an ice storm. She had leaned it against a guardrail, half-buried under snow. No ceremony. No hesitation. Just turned away and kept moving until the shape of it faded into the storm behind her.

Since then, she'd slept wherever she could: garages with oil stains frozen into the concrete, the back seats of cars with windshields shattered inward, porch swings wrapped in blankets pulled from upstairs closets, even a train platform once, her bag under her head and her bat balanced across her chest. She never stayed anywhere twice. Never stayed long enough for anything, or anyone, to find her.

If a house felt wrong, she left it. If a hallway felt watched, she changed direction. If the world went too still, she trusted that over anything else. She'd become something like fog. Visible for a moment, then gone.

Small stores kept her alive. Forgotten ones. The quieter, the better. A hair salon where she found two unopened water bottles meant for customers. A corner shop with stale cereal she ate dry by the handful. A hardware store where she pocketed faded hand warmers that still activated; she used both at once to try to feel warm.

Early on, she'd made the mistake of trying the mall.

Ten minutes was all she lasted.

The air inside felt wrong, dust and perfume and something metallic underneath. A stroller lay on its side near the escalator, a scrap of jacket caught in the broken teeth. No bodies. No blood. But something violent had moved through there. Something destructive. She hadn't stayed long enough to find out what. After that, she'd given up hope on finding Mary again.

Every night, she pressed her palm to the ground. Some nights: nothing. Others: a faint, inconsistent rumble, always nudging south. Patchy, unreliable, but real enough to follow.

By early evening, the sky dimmed into flat gray, and Faith spotted a shuttered laundromat ahead. Dark windows, door cracked open by the wind.

Good enough.

She tightened her scarf around her neck, adjusted her backpack, and slipped inside for the night.

The laundromat was colder inside than it looked from the street, but at least it wasn't windy. Faith pushed the door shut behind her, her fingers stiff around the metal handle, and walked past the dark row of washers until she reached the back wall. She tested the light switch with her knuckle.

A single overhead bulb flickered, then steadied into a dim yellow glow.

She let the relief settle quietly in her chest.

Faith slid her backpack off her shoulders and sat on the tile floor with her back against a dead dryer. She tugged her gloves off and tucked them into her coat pocket, exhaling into her hands until she could feel her fingers again. The room held a faint smell of detergent and dust, something old but clean enough to trust for one night.

She unzipped the front pocket of her bag and pulled out the notebook.

The cover was still stained from that night. The streak of dried wine looked darker in the weak light, like a bruise on the page. She ran her thumb along it out of habit, the familiar texture grounding her for a moment.

Then she opened it.

Cold air curled against her knuckles as she flipped to the next blank page. She reached for her pen, rubbed the tip between her palms, and breathed warm air over it until her reflection fogged the metal.

She pressed the nib to the paper.

Nothing.

She tried again, harder this time, dragging the pen in a trembling line across the page. The ink refused to move, frozen inside its casing, stiff as the air around her. She warmed it again, breath turning the metal slick.

She pressed down once more.

The nib snapped clean off.

Faith froze.

A tiny sting of frustration tightened across her ribs. She inhaled slowly, then exhaled through her nose, letting the cold settle over the disappointment like snow over a footprint. She pinched the paper at the corner and tried to tear out the page cleanly, but it crumbled at the edges, splitting into brittle flakes beneath her fingers.

She stared at what remained. Ragged, useless, broken in a way she couldn't fix.

Her chest tightened. Not panic. Something softer. A grief so small it barely made a sound inside her.

Faith ran her hands over the wine stains one more time, pressing her palms to the cover the way she used to press them to the earth, hoping for a pulse. The notebook felt thin, fragile, wrong.

She closed it gently as if it might fall apart, then she slid it back into her bag, zipped the pocket shut, and rested her forehead against her knees. The quiet pressed up against her like another layer of cold.

She didn't try to write again.

Outside, the sky had gone dark.

Faith lit a candle stub with shaking hands, shielding the tiny flame from the draft slipping through the laundromat's cracked door. The electric lights hummed overhead, steady but too bright for sleep. She reached up and clicked the wall switch off.

Darkness folded over the room except for the thin glow of her candle, trembling against the metal faces of the washers.

She settled on the floor between two machines, sliding her backpack beneath her head. The tile was cold even through her coat. She tightened her scarf, pulled her knees close, and took the pocket watch out again. Geno's picture flashed in the candlelight, warm, familiar, softer than she remembered. She held it in both hands, thumbs resting on the dent she always touched first.

The room was still. Too still.

Faith pressed her free hand to the floor, palm flat against the tile.

Nothing.

She exhaled slowly and let her head rest back against the dryer. The candle flickered beside her, haloing the air with the faintest warmth. She closed her eyes to drift, to let her body loosen just enough to forget how cold she was.

The hum arrived like a breath she didn't take.

At first, it was a whisper under her. Thin, almost imagined. She held still, waiting, hardly daring to breathe.

Then it grew.

A low pulse vibrated through the tile, up her back and into her bones. Not warm. Not gentle. A pressure, deep and heavy, like the world was turning its attention toward her. Faith's eyes opened, wide and startled. The vibration deepened, louder, stronger, until even she could feel it in her teeth. A hum so fierce it bordered on sound, pressing through the deaf quiet like something breaking in.

She sat up fast.

Headlights swept suddenly across the front windows, bright arcs of white and strobing blue slicing through the room. A car passing outside. Just a moment. Just a flash. And as fast as it came, it was gone.

But it lit everything.

The far corner of the laundromat flickered.

Faith stared.

On top of one of the washers sat an old TV. Unplugged, dust-webbed, dead for who knew how long... It snapped to life with a blue screen. Static rolled in thick waves. The candle flame stuttered and went out.

Faith froze, breath fogging in front of her.

The static shifted. Shapes formed in the noise. A face, then a jawline, then nothing. The image dissolved, returned, fell apart again.

A voice crawled through the distortion, warped and distant, like a radio broadcast buried under ice.

"Faith... I... can't help... love you..."

Her throat tightened. A tremor ran through her fingers.

The voice glitched, cut out, returned in a fractured whisper.

"...love..."

A tear slid down her cheek, hot against the cold.

Faith reached out toward the TV, trembling, her hand hovering inches from the vibrating metal of the washer beneath it. She didn't blink. Didn't breathe. Her fingertips shook like they were trying to touch something real, something warm.

The static snapped.

The screen went black.

The hum died with it.

Darkness rushed back in, absolute and immediate, leaving only her own heartbeat in the quiet.

Faith curled into herself, clutching the pocket watch tight against her chest. Her lips parted, shaping a name she hadn't dared to use aloud in weeks.

"Dad."

It slipped out without sound, warm only for the moment it lived on her mouth. And when it did, the candle sparked back to life.

Faith watched the candle flicker, then lay down on the cold tile, watch pressed to her heart, eyes still wet.

Sleep found her like a tide rushing in.

Chapter 13

Faith walked with her shoulders curled inward, boots sinking into the thin, steady layer of snow drifting across the road. Northern Delaware felt emptier than the places she'd passed before. Long broad spaces, low buildings, long stretches of nothing but white and wind. The hospital campus sat somewhere behind her now, swallowed by distance and winter.

Snowflakes clung to her eyelashes. Her breath blew out in thin, milky streams. Her nose had started running again, a slow, constant drip she wiped away on her sleeve. It made her cheeks sting. For a moment she wondered if she was getting sick, but the thought faded as quickly as it arrived. It was just the cold. It was always the cold. It had to be the cold.

The world around her felt muted in the deep winter cold. Pale sky, pale streets, pale houses half-buried in frost. Even movement seemed slow.

Something felt off. Not wrong, not dangerous... just... shifted. Like the day had tilted while she wasn't looking.

She stepped onto a patch of frozen pavement.

A vibration pulsed once under her boot.

Weak.

Directional.

Gone before she could lean into it.

Faith paused, tilting her head as if she could listen with more than her ears. The air stayed still. The road didn't move again. Snow drifted around her in soft, lazy spirals.

She sniffed hard and wiped her nose again.

Then she tightened her grip on her backpack strap and kept walking, breath curling behind her in the quiet.

The snowfall thickened as Faith reached the bend where the hospital roads gave way to wider stretches of Newark's outskirts. The buildings behind her thinned out, replaced by long sidewalks, bare trees, and the faint outline of brick college housing farther ahead.

She wiped her nose again, sleeve damp, breath curling up past her cheeks.

When she lifted her head, she froze.

A shape stood at the far end of the road.

Not close. Not even near enough to read as anything.

Just a dark, bulky silhouette on the horizon, half-blurred by drifting snow.

The figure was hunched, shoulders rounded beneath a heavy coat, hood pulled up. Something wrapped around the face, maybe a scarf, maybe just shadow. Its proportions weren't right. Too wide? Too bent? Too still?

For a moment she thought it might be an animal standing on its hind legs, or a person leaning awkwardly against the wind.

Then it shifted.

Or maybe the snowfall shifted.

She couldn't tell.

Faith kept walking. Same pace. Same rhythm.

Pretending her eyes hadn't snagged on that shape. Pretending her stomach hadn't flipped, sharp and sudden, like instinct trying to warn her of something she couldn't see.

Her breath grew heavy in her chest as she passed a set of empty bike racks. She didn't look back. Didn't want to. The world behind her felt stretched and desperate, snow swallowing everything in soft white sheets.

Up ahead, the road curved slightly to the left.

When she rounded it, the figure was gone.

Faith shifted her path without making it look intentional. She didn't speed up. Didn't stop. Just let her feet drift toward a side street that cut behind a medical office building. The snow was picking up, still light, but thick enough that the air had texture, like static building around her.

Behind the building, the world narrowed. Dumpsters, a loading dock, a stretch of cracked pavement. A perfect place to disappear for a moment. She kept her shoulders relaxed, pretending she was just choosing a better route out of the wind.

She didn't look back.

Not directly.

Every so often she tilted her head just slightly, using the blur at the edge of her vision to catch movement if there was any. But there was nothing behind her except drifting snow and the empty path she'd carved through it.

She slipped between buildings and crossed into a narrow alley that emptied near a strip of college housing. The wind tunneled through the gap, carrying loose flakes in little spirals around her boots. Her breath felt louder in her chest.

A small pedestrian bridge arched over a shallow creek just ahead. She stepped onto it, boots scraping lightly against the metal. Halfway across, something in her periphery tugged at her attention.

She glanced only with the corner of her eye.

A shape.

At the far end of the bridge.

Low, bulky, half-hidden behind the curtain of snow.

It was there for a heartbeat...

a shadow leaning, a hood maybe turned her way...

and then it blurred into the snowfall, gone as quickly as it appeared.

A cold twist pulled tight through her stomach.

Faith's pulse picked up.

She lifted her foot, and a faint vibration ran under the bridge.

One pulse.

Weak.

Directional.

Gone.

She didn't know if something was following her.

Or if the day itself was.

But she knew she didn't want to be out here anymore.

Faith's breath hitched in her chest, sharp and tight, as she stepped off the bridge. The cold in her stomach twisted into something hotter, sharper. Her fingers curled around the handle of her bat on her hip, skin stinging from the cold metal through her torn gloves.

She didn't look back.

She didn't want to see what might be there.

Her body moved before her thoughts caught up, a sudden burst forward, boots breaking into a run across the snow-slick sidewalk.

Her breath fogged hard in front of her, pulsing in frantic clouds. Each inhale burned her throat, raw and cold. Footsteps landed soft and muted. Her backpack slammed against her spine with every stride, each jolt tightening the fear already clawing up her ribs.

She cut down a narrow road that sloped between two rows of college rentals, identical duplexes split down the middle, half sunken porches, plastic trash bins frozen to the curb. The snow blurred everything, softening the edges, making each house look the same as the last.

Her lungs burned.

Her legs did too.

But she didn't stop.

Every few strides, she felt the urge to glance behind her, just a flick of the eyes, but the thought of what she might see tightened her throat even more. She kept her gaze forward, fixed on the next corner, the next porch, the next breath she had to force out.

Snow drifted harder now, blowing sideways in thin sheets that made her squint. Her vision tunneled. Her boots slipped once, nearly sending her skidding, but momentum kept her upright.

Then she saw it, a duplex at the end of the block with one door hanging crooked on its top hinge, porch light long dead, windows fogged from cold and neglect. Wide enough to hide inside. Empty enough to feel safe.

Her body locked onto it like instinct had chosen for her.

Faith sprinted the last stretch.

Her legs screamed.

Her chest felt like fire.

She stumbled up the small concrete step, gripping the railing to pull herself forward.

She shoved the door open with her shoulder and fell inside.

She slammed the door shut and leaned her full weight against it, trembling, bat still clutched at her side.

She didn't know if something had been behind her.

Or nothing at all.

The fear didn't care.

She'd made it.

That was enough.

She was afraid to look outside, at what might be there.

A shadow crossing the street.

Some figures in the distance.

But all she knew was the hard thump of her heart trying to beat its way out of her chest.

Faith pushed off the door slowly, her knees still trembling, and scanned the dim entryway. The duplex smelled like old carpet and cold drywall, empty long before the world ended. The living room opened on her left, shadows pooling behind abandoned furniture. A faded couch. A ring stained coffee table. A fallen bookshelf tipped forward like it had been knocked over in another lifetime.

Perfect.

She stepped toward it and planted her shoulder against the side, bracing her feet on the worn carpet. The wood scraped against the floor as she shoved, the vibration running up her arms. Inch by inch, she dragged it across the room until it blocked the door completely, wedged tight beneath the knob.

She tested it once with both hands.

Solid.

Heavy enough.

Good.

Her breath fogged as she backed away.

The windows along the front wall were thinly frosted, pale blue in the dying light. Snow drifted against the glass, piling softly at the corners. Faith moved toward them with her shoulders stiff, her body angled low like she expected something to be watching back.

Her fingers hovered over the cold glass.

Outside, the street was empty.

No movement.

No silhouette.

Just snow falling harder now, thick enough to blur the houses across the road into soft gray shapes.

The kind of snow that swallowed sound.

The kind that buried footprints in minutes.

The kind that hid everything.

Faith swallowed, throat tight.

She wiped her nose again.

Still just cold. Nothing more.

She checked the street a second time.

Then a third.

Still nothing.

But the fear didn't leave. It settled in her instead, slowly. Someone could've seen her. Someone could know she's in this house. Someone could be out there right now, hidden behind the white curtain swallowing the world.

Her breath grew shallow.

She stepped back from the window, backing deeper into the duplex, choosing a corner where the walls made her feel less exposed. The shadows lengthened with the falling dark, stretching across the floor like reaching branches.

She didn't light anything.

Didn't move the curtains.

Didn't touch the door again.

She just stood there, listening with her whole body, trying to feel vibrations through the soles of her boots, waiting for the world to tell her if she was safe.

It didn't.

The house stayed still.

The storm grew heavier.

The quiet pressed in.

Faith wrapped her arms around herself, breath shaking out of her in thin, quick bursts.

She wasn't sure which was worse, the idea that someone had followed her here…

…or the idea that someone now knew exactly where she'd be when the snow finally sealed her in.

Chapter 14

Faith woke with her cheek pressed against the cold hardwood, her body curled tight against the fallen bookshelf she'd dragged in front of the door the night before. For a moment she didn't know where she was. She only felt the sharp, small tremors running through her ribs, her breath slipping out in thick, pale curls.

The room was colder than any morning so far.

She lifted her head.

The windows were white.

Not frosted... but buried.

Snow pressed halfway up the glass, soft and heavy and unmoving, swallowing the world beyond it. The porch was gone. The street was gone. Everything had been erased by the storm.

Faith pushed herself upright, her muscles stiff and slow. Her coat crackled with frozen creases as she moved. She rubbed her arms through the sleeves, trying to coax a little warmth back into her skin.

She looked toward the front door.

Snow had climbed the outside steps and sealed the entry so completely the light around the frame had disappeared. She could've been underground for all she knew. Even if she unblocked the door, the storm had closed it from the other side.

She wasn't going anywhere today.

Maybe not tomorrow either.

She was trapped.

Her stomach pinched tight.

She reached for her backpack, fingers numb as she dragged it into her lap. Inside: one can. A half-full bottle of water. Nothing else but her clothes and her notebook. She dug in her pocket and thumbed the dent in the pocket watch.

Faith opened the can and ate the smallest spoonful she could manage, letting it melt on her tongue before swallowing. She counted the bites in her head. She closed the can and set it aside. A whole day's ration gone in seconds.

She moved to the fireplace, crouching in front of the black, empty grate. Her breath drifted into it like smoke. Last night's ashes sat dull and gray in a thin layer, barely warm enough to touch.

She gathered what little she had left for burning. Splintered trim from the broken bookshelf, a handful of junk mail she'd found in a drawer. She arranged them carefully, struck the match, and coaxed a small flame into life.

The fire crackled weakly, like it didn't want the responsibility.

Faith held her hands above it anyway.

The heat barely kissed her skin. The fire ate through the scraps too fast, smoke curling up the stone as if embarrassed.

She swallowed, throat tight. There wasn't much left in the house to burn. Not enough to last. Not for one night, let alone the weight of a blizzard still building outside.

She tucked her hands under her arms, leaning closer to the fragile flame.

Hopeless cold.

Hopeless storm.

Outside, snow kept climbing the windows.

Inside, the fire was already burning through the last of what she had left.

Faith pulled her knees to her chest, breath trembling in the cold.

She wasn't sure how long she could stretch one flame.

Or how long she was supposed to last.

Daylight didn't look like daylight anymore. It was blinding and white and impossible.

Even the night was bright. Between the moon in the sky and the snow on the ground, it kept it so bright she could barely sleep.

When Faith opened her eyes the next morning, the windows were a full wall of white. What little bit of sunlight had crept through the day before was completely blocked out, only glowing through the snow now. The house felt smaller than it had yesterday, colder too, like the storm was filling the rooms from the inside. Her breath hung thick in the air, refusing to fade.

Her stomach cramped hard.

Yesterday's ration hadn't lasted.

She crawled toward the fireplace, rubbing her hands together for warmth even though they'd stopped responding well to it. The cold in her fingers felt deep now, not just surface sting, like the bones themselves were chilling.

She needed fuel.

Anything that would burn.

Both for her, and for the fire.

Faith pushed herself to her feet and began scavenging.

She moved through the duplex room by room, breath fogging in front of her as she pried apart whatever she could. She snapped a closet shelf in half, then the loose slat from a bedroom vent. She pulled the legs off a small end table, using her body weight to crack them across her knee. Each piece she brought back to the living room like she was carrying offerings to something she hated.

She tore magazines from a nightstand. Stiff. Brittle.

She gathered junk mail from a hallway drawer.

She broke a picture frame, took the frame, left the glass.

By the time she had a pile, her vision blurred at the edges whenever she stood still. A dizziness rolled through her chest, slow and warm and wrong, hunger mixing with cold until it felt like her ribs might fold inward.

Faith knelt in front of the fireplace and fed it piece by piece, coaxing flame from nothing. The fire took reluctantly, shivering up the scraps in weak orange tongues. It gave off just enough heat for her to feel the difference between freezing and almost freezing.

It still wasn't enough.

She held her hands over the fire until her fingers tingled. Then she pulled them back and curled into herself, knees up, forehead resting against her coat.

Her chest tightened. Everything she'd been through started flooding back into her mind.

She needed something to focus on. Something to quiet the panic scraping up her ribs.

Faith reached for her backpack.

She pulled out her notebook, her last steady thing, and held it tight for a second, letting the worn cover warm between her palms. She opened to a blank page, breath fogging the paper.

The pen had broken days ago. The pages too worn and brittle to be of any use anymore.

Her breath hitched.

She tried turning the page, slowly, carefully... but the edges stuck together, frozen into thin, icy sheets. She pried at one corner. It tore like frostbitten skin, breaking apart into crumbling flakes between her fingers.

She looked down at the ruined page. Then at the fragile notebook that could barely survive the cold.

Her chest tightened again, sharper this time.

The fire behind her crackled weakly.

The storm pressed its weight against the windows.

Her fingers shook as she closed the notebook with both hands.

This was the moment her record began to die.

Faith rested her forehead on her knees again, breath trembling in the dim light, the notebook shut tight in her lap as the fire continued eating through the last pieces of the house she hadn't needed yet.

Faith sat with the notebook in her lap long after the fire lost its strength. Ash drifted lazily in the air around her. Thin, gray flakes that rose and fell like snow that had forgotten how to be cold. Every few seconds one would land on the cover, on her sleeve, or vanish in the air between breaths.

She stared at the notebook until her eyes burned.

She didn't need to try writing again.

She already knew.

Still… she slid a thumb under the top corner of one page and tugged, slow and careful, hoping this one might survive. Just one. Something she could fold, hide, keep. Something that could outlast the storm if she didn't.

The paper split before it even tore.

It disintegrated in her hands. Soft, brittle fragments breaking into dust across her palm.

Faith exhaled shakily.

That was her answer.

She closed the notebook, palms flat against the stained cover, and held it against her chest. The fire behind her sputtered, eating through its final scraps of wood. She didn't cry. Didn't panic. The cold had taken too much from her to leave room for that.

This was the last thing she had left of the world before.

So she would make it part of the world now.

Faith set the notebook beside her knees and reached for the kitchen drawer she'd pried open earlier. A single knife lay inside. Cheap metal, thin plastic handle. She pulled it out and held the blade over the fire until the metal glowed faintly, heat kissing her fingers even through her gloves.

Her hands trembled.

From hunger, from cold, from something deeper she didn't want to name.

She pushed her coat sleeve up to her elbow.

Her forearm looked small in the dim light. Pale, goose-pimpled, thin from weeks of walking and starving. She pressed the flat of the warm blade to her skin once, feeling the heat, letting her body register the shape of what she was about to do.

Then she carved.

A small heart first. Uneven, jagged, the curve trembling on one side where her hand shook too hard to keep the line smooth. She hissed an inhale through her teeth. Blood rose in a thin, bright seam.

Inside the heart, she carved the four letters of her father's name:

GENO

Each stroke shallow but raw.

Each letter a tiny wound she refused to stop making.

When it was done, she dipped two fingers into the ash at the edge of the dying fire. The flakes clung to her skin. She pressed them gently into the cuts, rubbing until the gray powder filled the fresh grooves.

Her arm burned.

But it was hers now.

Faith swallowed and lowered the knife again.

Below the heart, she carved a spiral.

The same spiral she drew as a child,

the same shape she traced in dirt,

the same one that lived in the hum beneath the world.

A single curling line that wound inward once before opening into two clean arms.

Simple, symmetrical, ancient.

Exactly like the one she used to doodle when she needed to feel safe.

The same one her father had a tattoo of.

The cut stung sharply as she completed the final turn.

She rubbed ash into this one too, until the lines grew dark and permanent.

When she finally put the knife down, her breath shook from somewhere deep in her ribs. Her arm throbbed, warm beneath the cold air, the skin angry and swollen, but marked. Marked in a way nothing could erase.

Faith picked up her notebook again.

She held it a moment.

Then fed the first page into the fire.

It curled quickly in the weak flame, paper turning black then orange then nothing. She fed another. And another. Slowly. Page by fragile page, she kept the fire alive with the only record of her life she had left until the warmth finally reached her cheeks again.

Ash drifted around her, soft and weightless.

And Faith sat still in its fall, her father's name burning under her skin, the spiral beneath it humming faintly in her bones.

Chapter 15

Faith didn't remember falling asleep.

She only remembered waking, if this could be called waking. She was slumped against the wall beside the dead fireplace, her whole body curled as tight as her bones allowed. The ache was already deep inside her body.

The room felt darker than before.

Colder than before.

She lifted her head an inch. It felt like it took every drop of energy that wasn't frozen to do it.

The fire was gone.

A single gray thread of smoke drifted from the dead ember and disappeared. Faith stared at it for a long time before she realized she wasn't blinking. Her eyes were too tired even for that.

She didn't move to save it.

She couldn't.

Her arms wouldn't listen.

She reached for her backpack with slow, clumsy fingers.

Empty.

She'd known that before looking, but seeing it still made her chest tighten.

The water had frozen in the bottle.

She lifted it, stared at the ice, and set it down again.

Even snow hurt to swallow now.

She drew her coat tighter around herself, though the fabric felt stiff and brittle, like folding paper around a dying animal. Her hands shook when she pulled them back into her sleeves. The shaking didn't stop, even when she pressed them under her arms. Her skin felt far away from her.

A thin rime of frost had begun to creep along the inside of the window behind her, tracing pale, delicate patterns like spiderwebs. Snow pressed up past the midway point of the glass now. No street. No sky. No world beyond the cold.

She was sealed in.

Her throat felt scraped raw.

Her lips were pale and cracked.

Her breath fogged only a little now, weak and thin.

Faith blinked once. Then again, slower.

Her lashes brushed frost from the corner of her eye.

She wasn't sure she could stay awake much longer.

She wasn't sure she wanted to.

Her breath shivered out of her in a soft, uneven cloud.

Her eyes drifted half-closed.

The walls seemed to lean, then soften, then fold inward like shadows.

Faith let her chin fall to her chest. The cold crept further into her, quiet and patient.

And as the last bit of light slipped out of the room, dragging the day with it, she let her mind slide under.

Not into rest,

   but into something deeper,

      darker,

         and dream-heavy.

She didn't fight it.

She didn't have the strength.

Everything went gray.

The gray closed over her like a tide.

Cold at first.

Then thick.

Then strangely warm.

Faith drifted down through it, weightless, untethered, until she wasn't sure if her eyes were open or shut.

Something glowed. A faint orange curl of light flickered along her arm. She blinked and the ash tattoos she'd carved days ago weren't lines anymore.

They were moving.

The name GENO pulsed once, like a heartbeat. Then the letters unbent themselves, straightened, curved, and reformed. Not as word, but as features.

Her father's cheekbones took shape first.

Then the bridge of his nose, faint as pencil.

Then the rough shadow of his beard.

His face flickered across her skin like a sketch being drawn in real time.

She gasped, but no sound left her.

The spiral beneath the name swirled, tightened, and became the outline of his jaw. The heart around GENO closed itself, forming the hollow of his ear. Ash lifted like dust caught in sunlight.

And then he spoke.

"Faith."

The word didn't come from a mouth.

It didn't come from the air either.

It wrote itself, letter by letter, across her forearm as she heard it, the ink appearing in time with the sound.

F A I T H

She wasn't sure if she was reading or hearing. Maybe both? Both felt impossible. But both felt right.

Her father's face tilted toward her, soft the way she remembered, the way he looked in her locket.

"Sweetheart," the letters formed. "You've gotten so strong."

New words traced themselves slowly, painfully, curling across her skin like warm blades. She didn't mind the pain, not from him.

"I'm proud of you."

"I'm sorry for everything I couldn't fix."

"I'm here."

Faith tried to reach him. Her arm didn't move. Her fingers felt carved from ice.

The warmth of him flickered, and started to dissolve.

His face sagged into charcoal. The lines blurred. The spiral under him twisted.

The shadow behind him grew.

A tall, wrong-shaped silhouette rose from the curling ash, stretching up her arm like spilled ink deciding to become a person. Its head was too low. Its arms too long. Its posture bent forward like something halfway between a man and an animal.

The warm glow dimmed. The cold returned.

The shadow stepped closer. Off of her arm and into the dark, cold, suffocating room that had swallowed her.

Faith's breath caught in her chest. The silhouette leaned in, filling her vision, bending its shape in ways bones couldn't.

Then it lunged.

Faith stumbled backward into nothing... Into air.

Until her legs found way beneath her, a stairwell spiraled upward around her.

Endless. Narrow. Wooden steps slamming under her feet in rhythm with her heartbeat...

She sprinted up the stairs. The shadow thundered after her, each impact shaking the staircase, its form ballooning, stretching, filling the space behind her. Its breath was hot on her neck. Its fingers brushed her coat.

She ran until her legs didn't belong to her. Ran until the stairs bent sideways. Ran until her vision snapped white.

She closed her eyes and screamed... But no sound came out.

When she opened them again, warm yellow light spilled through red shutters.

Faith stood outside a house she'd never seen but somehow recognized. The snow beneath her feet melted to wet grass. Frost slid off the windows and turned into drifting sheets of paper.

Dozens.

Hundreds.

All blank.

All fluttering like birds with no wings.

She stepped forward.

A man paced inside the house.

Big, heavy-shouldered, bearded, tattoos coiling up his forearms.

Eyes wild.

Face red.

Mouth open in a scream she couldn't hear.

He slammed his palms on a desk.

Pages scattered.

He grabbed a pen, scribbled, tore the page out, threw it.

Grabbed another.

Scribbled again.

Ripped.

Threw.

He didn't see her.

Faith pressed her hand against the window. The glass was warm. Too warm, like touching someone's skin.

The man spun toward her...

...and for one impossible second their eyes met.

"You shouldn't be here..." He looked puzzled, "You should be..."

Faith stared,

trying to understand him,

but the pages around him twisted,

the shutters slammed,

the light went black.

The shadow figure was there again, behind her.

Closer.

So close she felt its shape bend over her.

She cowered down, tears of ice poured from her eyes and shattered the floor beneath her feet. She collapsed to the floor of the duplex.

The cold returned in a single wave. Faith lay on her side, breath thin, eyelids too heavy to lift. The fire was dead. The air was freezing.

Her arm throbbed where her father's name had once lived warm.

She mouthed the words, just once, just barely...

"I'm sorry, Daddy..."

Not a sound escaped.

The gray folded in.

The cold closed over her.

Faith stopped fighting.

Chapter 16

Faith felt movement before she felt anything else. Some kind of dragging.

Her body shifting across the floor inch by inch.

A dull scrape under her coat.

Heat somewhere close, close enough that her cheek stung from the sudden change.

She forced her eyes open a slit.

A shape hovered over her.

Big coat.

Shoulders bent forward.

Nothing clear.

Just the outline of someone working hard to get her closer to the fireplace.

His breath showed in short bursts.

White in the dark.

She didn't hear a voice, but his mouth moved as he pulled her another few inches. "Damn you're heavy…"

She couldn't lift her head.

Couldn't answer.

Couldn't even hold on to the moment long enough to understand it.

Warmth brushed her back as he propped her nearer to the fire.

A blanket or coat moved over her legs.

His hands were quick. Rough, but careful.

Her eyes slipped closed again before she meant them to.

The silhouette leaned over her, adjusting something she couldn't see.

Then everything went dark.

Faith came back slowly. Not all at once. Just a thin slice of awareness, enough to feel heat on one side of her face and something solid beneath her cheek.

Her head rested in someone's lap.

A heavy coat.

Scratchy fabric.

She couldn't lift it.

Couldn't even turn into it.

The fire was close. She could feel it in faint pulses against her skin, not enough to warm her, just enough to remind her what warmth used to be.

Her vision stayed blurry.

Shapes.

Shadows.

The outline of a hand moving near her mouth.

Something touched her lips.

Wet.

Warm.

Salt.

Her throat tightened on instinct.

A spoon.

She swallowed without meaning to.

The man above her shifted, adjusting her slightly. She saw the shape of his mouth move, slow, careful words she couldn't hear. "Good… there you go…"

Another sip.

He steadied her head with one hand, thick fingers bracing her jaw so the broth didn't spill. His breath showed in the cold air, drifting across her vision in short white curls.

She took another swallow.

And another.

Her body relaxed into it, too weak to do anything else.

His mouth moved again.

She didn't understand the words.

Just the shape of them.

Her eyes closed on their own.

The spoon lowered.

His hand eased her head back into the cradle of his lap, steady and certain in a way nothing else in her world had been for weeks.

The fire crackled beside them. Soft, distant, almost imaginary.

Faith slipped under again.

Faith drifted back up again, slow and unsteady, like something pulling her toward the surface. She didn't open her eyes fully. Just enough to see a smear of orange light and the outline of a figure sitting beside her.

Her head rested on a pillow now.

The fire was close.

Close enough that she could feel heat against her cheek.

Real heat.

Not memory.

She blinked.

The silhouette leaned a little, hands resting on his knees.

The light behind him kept his face in shadow.

His mouth moved. "Good… you're awake."

He waited a moment, like he was giving her time to catch up. Then asked, "What's your name?"

Faith lifted her hand.

It shook once, then steadied just enough to shape the sign.

"Faith."

Her fingers barely finished the motion before her arm dropped back to the blanket.

The figure nodded, breath showing briefly in the air between them.

His mouth shaped more words.

Careful.

Measured.

"I'll have to work on that some…" He hesitated just long enough for her to read it. "Can you read lips?"

She nodded once, small and slow.

He shifted a little closer, enough that she could see the outline of his hair, his shoulders, the way he held himself. Solid, warm, enormous in the firelight.

His mouth formed the last words she saw that night, just as she slipped back to sleep.

"My name is Justice."

About the Author

D. R. Long lives in Delaware with his dog, Girl. He believes a story should be worth its salt; judged for its substance rather than its aesthetic.

If you'd like to see my books in your local bookstore or library, ask for D. R. Long by name. Reader requests matter more than you think.

Find other works at drlongwrites.com.

FROM THE WORLD OF D. R. LONG

An excerpt from the novel:

THE MONSTERS WE ARE

Chapter 1

The City Bleeds

The city hadn't stopped bleeding since the cloaks came off. Five years later and the wounds still hadn't scabbed. You could see it in the way the neon hit puddles, in the way the 'normals' lit their cigarettes, in the way everyone pretended the monsters had just appeared, instead of always being there.

From the window above the alley, Nightmare City shimmered in red and blue like a crime scene that never got cleaned. Neon signs blinked Morse code for the hopeless, advertising sins that didn't even need advertising anymore. A snake-girl haggled over fruit with a vendor who pretended he wasn't terrified of being the next meal. A pig-cop leaned against his cruiser, sugar dust clinging to his tusks. A couple of humans hurried past, eyes down, pretending not to notice the fangs, claws, and tails of the monsters around them.

<They used to hide. Now they don't. Lucky bastards. I never got that choice.>

A tram screeched by, spraying puddles onto a billboard that used to read Bridgework Collective: Building Tomorrow Together. The paint had peeled until it just said Collective. <Fitting.> The future got left behind somewhere around year three, right after the riots and before the curfews stopped meaning anything.

<You can see a lot from up here. Lies mostly. This city tells a new one every hour.>

Inside, Lou Fisk sat at his desk in the dark, eyes half-lidded. The lighter snapped, a small, tired sound. The cigarette glowed to life between his fingers, smoke drifting upward, curling into the light. He watched the photograph sitting beside his ashtray. A little girl, missing a front tooth, the picture creased from years of fingers tracing it.

He stared until the smoke blurred her face. Didn't blink. Didn't look away.

<Five years, and the city still takes more than it gives.>

Rain started again, soft at first, then harder, like someone upstairs decided to rinse the blood off the sidewalks. Didn't matter. It'd all be painted red again by morning.

The rain didn't stop. It just settled into a rhythm, same as the city. Lou walked over and cracked the blinds wider. Neon slid through the gaps, red and blue bars crawling across the floor and over the mess on his desk.

The radio mumbled from the corner, a talk host shouting about protests in the Normal Zone. More words about purity, progress, and peace. Lou shut it off. The silence hit quick and heavy.

<Always the same shit on the radio... Doesn't matter, I can't see the lies on the radio.>

That was the curse of it. He could spot a lie in a heartbeat. He could see the shift in someone's eyes, the shimmer that ran across their face when the truth slipped, but the rest of the world got to lie from a safe distance. The radio. The news. The politicians. All untouchable.

The phone started ringing. Lou didn't move. He watched it flash three times before the machine kicked in. Static, then a voice.

"Mr. Fisk, uh... I heard you take work. My cat's gone missing. Been gone a week now. I-"

He hit delete before it finished.

<Call the fire department, bud.>

He stood, joints cracking from too many hours in the same chair. The bottle of middle level whiskey waited where he'd left it. He poured a shot into a glass that didn't need cleaning anymore and took it in one go. The burn crawled down, sharp and familiar.

A photo of his daughter sat by the ashtray. He picked it up, thumb rubbing the crease that ran across the middle. She always smiled back, tooth missing, forever caught between laughs. He stared at it until the guilt started to push through, then set it down again.

He pulled a long drag from his cigarette, watched the cherry flare, and used it to light another before crushing the first out. Smoke folded in on itself and hung over the desk like fog.

He used to tell himself he'd done everything he could. Now he just told himself to stop thinking about it. <Still, never gets any easier living without her.>

On the side of the desk, a stack of old files leaned like bad memories. He grabbed the one on top. The tab read Unsolved.

He flipped it open, looked at the first page, then the next. <Nothing new to see. Nothing ever was.>

The rain had turned to mist, the kind that hung in the air instead of falling. Lou's office smelled like smoke, whiskey, and the kind of paper that's been waiting too long to matter. The ashtray overflowed, the glass sat empty, and the file in front of him hadn't learned anything new.

He dragged one last pull from the cigarette, stubbed it out, and let the room go still. The quiet settled heavy again, the way it always did before something knocked.

Then he heard it. Footsteps on the stairs.

Slow ones. Careful. Each step landing just a little too soft, like whoever it was didn't want to be heard but didn't know how to disappear. The old boards creaked anyway; they always told on you.

Lou didn't move. He watched the strip of light under the door. The rain outside threw faint reflections through the blinds, bending them into bars. Smoke curled between them and made shadows that almost looked alive.

<Could be a bill collector. Could be worse.>

He slid the revolver into the top drawer of his desk and pushed the papers back over it like a promise. Not hidden, not brave, just close enough to the skin to feel right. Then he poured another slug of whiskey, watched the light bend through the glass, and swallowed it down slow.

The footsteps stopped outside the door. He could see the silhouette of high heels in the light under the door.

<People only knock for two reasons. One's trouble. The other's worse... They want help.

Three light taps. A pause. The handle turned halfway, then stopped, then moved again. Lou let his empty glass sit on the blotter and stood slow, like he was stretching muscles that hadn't moved in a while.

"Office hours," he said, not looking to the door.

The door knob rattled anyway.

"Come back tomorrow, toots! Office is closed!" Lou's voice started to raise when he heard the soft cry from outside.

"Please, Mister Fisk... You're the only one that can help me!"

<Shit. I know what that means...>

Chapter 2

Rain and Trouble

The knock came again. Softer this time, like whoever was behind it wasn't sure they belonged there. Lou looked at the glass on the desk, took a deep breath, and walked to the door.

He opened it halfway.

She filled the doorway like the city had built it for her. Rain clung to her coat, darkening the fabric until it gleamed under the hall light. Her hair stuck to her cheeks in wet strands, eyes too sharp for someone that lost, lips the color of secrets you don't tell twice.

She was gorgeous in a way that didn't make sense in a place like this. Too polished, too clean, like someone had dropped her in from a better dream. For a second, Lou forgot to breathe.

<Snap out of it, Lou. She's just another dame!>

Then the city found its voice again behind her. Tires hissing through water, sirens stretching thin in the distance, a flickering sign somewhere down the block. The sound broke the spell.

For a second, neither of them spoke.

"Lou Fisk?" she asked. Voice steady, but the edges trembled.

"That's the rumor."

She let out a breath that was almost a laugh. "You take cases?"

<They always start with rain and trouble. Usually in that order.>

He opened the door the rest of the way and stepped aside. She crossed the threshold slow, the smell of rain and perfume trailing after her. Water hit the floor one drop at a time, tiny dark circles spreading like secrets.

The coat was expensive, the shoes weren't. Her nails were chipped down to the color of old wine. She looked like she'd run out of ways to keep pretending everything was fine... and when she said, "I'm fine," Lou saw the shimmer cross her face.

<She's lying.>

That was his gift. He appeared pretty normal compared to most of the mutants in Nightmare City, but he was still one of them. When people lied, he saw it. Not words, not colors, just a faint ripple that slid over their skin like heat off asphalt. Didn't tell him the truth, only that the truth wasn't what he was hearing. The rest he had to guess at like everyone else.

He nodded toward the chair opposite his desk. "That one doesn't bite."

She sat. It creaked, held, and sighed like the rest of the room.

Lou closed the door, poured two fingers of whiskey into his own glass, and waited for her to start lying again.

The rain still clung to her. Small circles seeped into the carpet under her. The smell of her perfume hung in the air, mixing with the smoke and the old whiskey on Lou's breath until the whole room smelled like confession. She crossed her legs, leaned forward a little, and tried to look composed. The chair complained under her.

"I'm Maya Joyner, and my father's dead," she said.

Lou didn't flinch.

He'd heard the words before. From widows, from suspects, from people who wished it was true.

He only watched her eyes.

"Jonas Joyner," she added, as if the name should mean something.

<It did.> The papers called him a bridge-builder, the kind of man who made peace for profit. Lou called that a middleman with better lighting.

"The cops say it was business," she went on. "A deal gone bad."

"Yeah, they always say that. Fucking pigs," Lou reached for his whiskey. He took a sip, then let the silence pull at her. When she filled it, her voice was smaller.

"They won't investigate. The Board's already replacing him."

<That part's true.>

Her eyes wavered. He caught the shimmer when she said, "I don't care why it happened."

<Liar.>

She looked down at her hands, rubbing her thumb across the rim of a wet glove.

"I just want to know who did it."

<Truth. Interesting.>

Lou set the glass down and let it roll a little on the desk.

"You sure you're in the right place, Miss Joyner? I do lost things. Cheating husbands, missing pets, bad investments. Murder's a little high-rent for me."

She smiled, small, careful. "I'm not hiring you to avenge him, Mr. Fisk. I just need someone who can see what the police won't."

He studied her, she was telling the truth. "And what makes you think I can?"

"Because you see lies," she said. Not a question. A statement. Also the truth.

Lou felt something tighten in his chest. "You've been doing your homework."

"I've been desperate," she said, and the shimmer didn't show this time. That one was the truth.

Outside, thunder rolled close enough to shake the windowpane. The light from the blinds striped her face, cutting it into fragments of gold and shadow.

She reached into her coat and pulled out a folded newspaper clipping. Jonas Joyner smiling for cameras beside a group of Board members. The headline read Bridgework Collective Celebrates Five Years Since Cloaks-Off Unity Accord.

"There's footage from that night," she said. "The gala at the Neutral Hall. The cameras went dark for seven minutes. When they came back, my father was gone."

Lou took the clipping, scanned it, and tossed it back onto the desk.

"Seven minutes is a long time to be gone."

"I'll pay you for your time," she said. "Whatever it costs."

<Everyone says that part. None of them mean it. But this one comes from serious money.>

He nodded toward the window. "You've got a lot of nerve walking through this neighborhood alone."

Her smile almost reached her eyes. "I didn't come here alone."

Lou glanced past her, through the blinds, but the street outside was empty except for the rain. When he looked back, she was still smiling, the kind of smile that made promises it didn't intend to keep.

She didn't rush to speak again.

The rain filled the gap for her, tapping the glass, soft and even. Lou poured another drink, slower this time, and set the bottle between them. She didn't touch it, just watched him.

When she finally leaned forward, her voice came low, careful.

"Then tell me what it takes to make you listen."

She reached inside the coat, pulled out an envelope, and slid it across the desk. The paper left a dark streak where it passed through a small puddle of rainwater.

Lou looked at it, but didn't reach for it. "You don't even know what I charge."

"I don't care," she said.

<Hmm... Truth again.>

Her eyes caught the light from the blinds, and for a second, he forgot what he was supposed to do. The room felt thicker, the air heavier, like it was waiting for him to answer.

He meant to push the envelope back, but his hand didn't move. The skin on his arms tingled, just a whisper, like static building before a storm. She wasn't touching him, wasn't even close, but he felt her in the air between them, warm, steady, persuasive. Her perfume seemed to fold around him, almost seductive.

He took a drink instead of answering. "Tell me what you're really paying for."

"I told you," she said. "Answers."

Lou looked at the envelope again. He should've asked more questions. He should've told her no. But she was telling the truth.

Instead he reached out, fingers brushing the edge of the paper. The smell of her perfume mixed with the smoke; it filled his head like a memory he didn't own.

"I'll look into it," he heard himself say.

<The second I said it, I knew she'd made me. Hook, line, and good intentions.>

Maya smiled then, a small, knowing thing. She stood, smoothed her coat, and left a faint hand print on the edge of his desk.

"I'll be in touch," she said, and the way she said it felt like a promise and a warning both.

<I know you will.>

He looked down at his hand. The fingers that touched the envelope still tingled.

The door clicked shut soft, the sound smaller than it should've been.

For a second, Lou just sat there, listening to the echo fade down the hall. The smell she left behind filled the room, perfume and rain, the kind that stuck to the air instead of the skin.

He breathed it in without meaning to, then frowned at himself. It reminded him of the kind of nights he used to believe in. The kind that ended with someone still beside you when the sun came up.

<Should've known better by now.>

He reached for the envelope, half expecting it to feel warm from her hands. The paper was dry. He thumbed through the cash inside, real money, crisp, too clean for this part of town. A business card slipped out and landed face-up on the desk.

Bridgework Collective. Embossed, expensive stock. A handwritten number on the back with the name Maya underneath.

Lou turned it over twice, like it might explain itself if he stared long enough.

<Great. A Board job wrapped in perfume. Just what I needed.>

He set the card aside, poured what was left in the bottle into his glass, and took a long swallow. The whiskey hit the back of his throat and stayed there, like it didn't want to leave either.

He pulled out and lit another cigarette, the cherry flaring in the dark. Smoke rolled up toward the ceiling and caught the light in faint ribbons, like ghosts that didn't know which way was out.

The chair across from him was still warm. The scent still lingered.

<She left the door open just long enough to let the trouble in.>

He leaned back, watching the smoke fade, waiting for it all to smell like the city again.

Dive deeper into the Spiral - scan the code below!